Making Big Decisions

Sunrise Beach - Book 4

Charlotte Golding

Copyright © 2022 Charlotte Golding and Sweet River Publishing

All rights reserved.

No part of this book may be reproduced in any form or by any electronic or mechanical means, including information storage and retrieval systems. Publisher expressly prohibits any form of reproduction.

———

This is a work of fiction. Any references to names, characters, organizations, places, events, or incidents are either products of the author's imagination or are used fictitiously.

The Sunrise Beach Series

This series is all about Stella Britton and her life after scandal and divorce. Stella is starting over in a new town away from the city she once loved. She hopes to come to love the small beach town she's chosen and that she and her daughter will find a new life away from the whispers.

Relationships have ups and downs, ins and outs. Stella knows this all too well. Now she'll navigate difficulties with her daughter, cherish a new friendship she didn't expect, and learn to depend on her neighbors.

Can she do this new life thing? Of course! Will it be easy? Not on your life!

Making Big Decisions

Sunrise Beach - Book 4

Charlotte Golding

Chapter One

Stella had sworn that she wouldn't do this again so soon. She couldn't believe that once again, she was facing a familiar sense of anxiety, a mountain of work that she had climbed before. Had she not already poured her heart out? Part of her wasn't sure she still had it in her, given her experiences as of late, but she was determined to prove that self-doubting voice wrong once again, like she had so many times in the past three years.

She was going to do another art exhibit.

The canvas in front of her window mocked her. Every color she added looked off, though perhaps that was just the fact that she rarely painted in her bedroom and the lighting was different. Angela Goff had told her to try something different, something new that she hadn't done before. And when an artist that successful said jump, well, Stella could only ask how high.

It wasn't as though she wasn't looking forward to doing another exhibit. On the plus side, this one would be minimal work on her part, or so Angela had promised. She had teams that would take care of everything. All Stella had to do was create a new, stunning body of work to be featured next to that of one of the most famous, not to mention her personal favorite, artists in the region. She'd toured, been featured in museums, made the kind of money Stella could only dream of making, all because of her art. And here she was, giving Stella free publicity, counsel, and, if she were to dare to let herself dream, friendship.

The challenges were harder to think of than they were to execute, Stella thought. Angela had told her that she should do things that were outside her comfort zone, but she'd built her entire artistic career on being forced out of that place. Her comfort zone had been her home in Atlanta with her husband, who wasn't a convicted felon, and their beautiful, stunning daughter, who had an enormous college fund and everything she could ever want. When that had been taken away, all she'd had was art, and her paintings had changed fairly dramatically. Now, she was struggling to find anything she could change in her daily life that might compete with that feeling.

She'd tried waking in the middle of the night to paint, but she'd just been too sleepy to even begin. Next, she'd limited her supplies, telling herself she couldn't wash her brush between colors or that she could only use blue and white. Mostly, that had just made a mess. Now, she was trying to make herself physically uncomfortable in the hopes of tapping into something new. Her bedroom was small and cramped, and in order to see the beach out the window, she had to crane her neck in a way that was beginning to hurt. Though she failed to see how this was going to somehow produce a better work of art, she was trying her

Making Big Decisions

best. She wanted to see in herself what Angela saw in her, too, after all.

Just as Stella decided she needed a break to do some shoulder stretches, her phone buzzed in her pocket, and she knew immediately who it was. Felicia never woke this early. Her mother-in-law, Gwen, never called her before dinner, and Kelsey was getting ready for school.

"Angela," she greeted, trying to keep the embarrassing excitement from her voice, "good morning. How are you?"

"I'm swell," she replied. "I've been up all night wrestling with a piece for the gallery. I think I've finally cracked it, though. I'm hating it less the more I look at it." Angela had been using her gallery as her own studio, since she didn't trust leaving her paintings in her hotel room. Not to mention, painting could get messy, and she didn't particularly want to pay them for a new carpet when she spilled oil paint on theirs.

Stella laughed. "I'm sure it's incredible. I can't wait to see it."

"Well, I was going to go home," she said, "but I suppose, if you wanted to meet up for a while, I could stick around." Thankful for the fact that Angela couldn't see her face, Stella broke into a wide grin.

"I would love that."

"There's one condition!" Stella paused, waiting for the other shoe to drop. "I need caffeine, and a lot of it. If you want me to stay, you'll bring me a red-eye."

Stella didn't have the heart to tell her she had no idea what that was. "Done," she replied.

Stella was lucky that the teenager who worked at the local Starbucks knew that a red-eye was apparently a cup of black coffee with a shot of espresso, a combination that made Stella feel like she was sweating just thinking about it. She liked her coffee, but she couldn't handle much more than one cup without her heart beating like she'd run a marathon. People who drank coffee like Angela did baffled her, and she was careful not to get the two drinks mixed up on the way to the gallery.

"Hi," she greeted, barely able to get the word out before Angela was taking the coffee from her and leading her to the studio in the back. She'd trusted her with the spare key, just for the purpose of locking up after she was done, but she was beginning to wonder if that had been a poor choice. She practically lived here now. "When was the last time you slept?"

Angela made a dismissive sound in the back of her throat and turned her canvas to show Stella. "Look at this. It's missing something, don't you think?"

Stella didn't know whether she agreed with that, but she knew that wasn't what Angela wanted to hear. Artists always wanted to hear that they were right, even about their mistakes. She pondered the painting for a moment, taking her time with it as Angela had done with so many of her own. Angela's paintings were so different from Stella's that she often wondered what had even drawn Angela to her art in the first place. Where Stella tended to depict landscapes, most recently of the beach, Angela's were all over the place. She barely ever painted the same subject twice. It seemed as though there was nothing she couldn't make look perfect, whether it was a landscape or a person or an abstract collection of colors and shapes.

Mostly, though, ever since her museum tour, Angela

tended to focus on colorful, almost magical depictions of everyday things. She painted subjects like Stella did, mundane settings and sometimes even household objects, but she used vibrant rainbows of oil paint to make them look surreal. Stella wanted to live in a world that looked like an Angela Goff painting.

This one, however, was different. It was neutral in color, with bases of tans and muted pastels. She could make out a bench, but not much else.

"What are you going for, here?" she asked, hoping that the question sounded more curious than judgmental. Angela sighed.

"This is the smallest town where I've stayed put in a long time," she admitted unhelpfully. "There's a certain vibe to it. I can't really put my finger on it. It's warm, but also sort of bland. Things are slow, but not in an unpleasant way. I really like it, but I could certainly never live in North Carolina. It's just too boring."

Stella nodded. "You know, coming from a town like Atlanta, I thought the same thing at first, but there's more to it than just what's on the surface. You can't judge a book by its cover."

"But I can judge a town by its complete lack of museums, history, and cultural significance."

Stella winced. "I just like to think of it as a blank canvas. In the big city, things happen to you, but in a place like this, people happen to the town. You can really feel like you make a difference here."

Angela seemed to light up at that. "Poetry," she replied. "I want to see that feeling on a canvas. Can you capture it?"

"I'm not sure," Stella admitted. "I don't really know what it would look like. It's just a feeling."

"And you," she said, "are an artist. That's your entire job, capturing feelings and turning them into something to look at. Just play around with it."

Stella sat down across from where Angela had finally allowed herself to collapse onto the stool. "Can I be totally honest?" Angela nodded. "I don't know how to paint like you do. When I paint with my feelings, I start with an object, and the emotions just come up naturally. Painting an emotion alone? I wouldn't even know where to start."

Angela nodded. "Close your eyes for me."

Reluctantly and somewhat doubtfully, Stella obeyed. "Okay. What are we doing?"

"Hush. I'm trying something." Angela lowered her voice to a soothing, slow tone that made Stella think of the time just after Jeff had left her, when she'd begun listening to a lot of guided meditations to try to get a handle on the anxiety that had followed. "Now, pull up that feeling, of feeling important in the smallness of the town. What's the emotion that makes it important?"

Stella sighed. "I suppose it's feeling loved and supported. In Atlanta, no one cared that I painted. I'd done a little community college class that had a big student gallery at the end of the semester, and barely anyone I knew came. This was years ago, of course, but it had hurt. I'd invited everyone I worked with, all the women I thought were my friends from the PTA. Here, when people found out I had put together a gallery, everyone wanted to help. There wasn't a single person I knew that didn't come by, at least for a little while. It felt like it mattered that I had done the gallery at all."

"What color is that feeling?"

Stella tried hard not to laugh, but she couldn't help but crack a smile. "What color is it?"

"Just play along."

She searched her mind for an answer, but it didn't come easily. "I guess it's a lot," she replied. "The beige of the sand on the beach. The orange of the walls of the gallery. The white of the fog on the roads from the ocean every morning when I go jogging. I think of a lot of colors."

"Good. The next time you sit down to paint, I want you to only use colors that evoke a strong emotional response like that. Try to mix your paints until they're perfect, just like they are in your memories."

"But what should I paint?"

Angela shrugged. "That'll come to you! I promise. I rarely know what I'm going to paint until I sit down and start to feel it out. You rely so much on planning. I know you're a mother and you've had your life uprooted by the divorce, so planning makes you feel safe. I want you to explore the mess side of things. I find that the best things come to those of us who fly by the seat of our pants."

Stella nodded. "I can try it." Truthfully, she was skeptical. She'd tried that before, sitting down to a canvas with no plan, and it had never gone well. Usually, she would just sit there and stare at the blank paper until she grew so frustrated with herself that she didn't even feel like painting at all.

Still, she'd grown as an artist more in the past few months than she had in years of classes, and she owed that almost entirely to how challenging the year had been. Her first exhibit had only been so robust with her own art because Adele had dropped out at the last minute and Stella had needed to fill the walls with something, and those paintings had sold well. She'd only begun painting so much because of the fact that she could no longer rely on Jeff for income. Everything that had happened to her had made her a better artist, and she was finally ready to see how far she could push this growth. No one had ever seen her in this way before, and she was excited to finally have the type of friend she'd so often longed for.

Chapter Two

Stella only invited Angela to her home once, but after that first visit, it seemed to become a routine. She imagined it was lonely in the hotel, but there was a part of Stella that hoped Angela was hanging around because she wanted to, rather than simply because there was nothing else to do. Angela would come over after dinner a few nights a week to discuss art, everything from the exhibit they were working on to their favorite artists and paintings. Angela knew all kinds of artists Stella had never heard of. She'd been to so many places and had so much advice that Stella couldn't think of a better way to spend her evening than just soaking up everything Angela wanted to share with her.

It couldn't have come at a better time, either, as Kelsey had been out of the house more and more lately. Unlike past instances in which her daughter had spent more time out than around the house, they weren't fighting. In fact, Stella thought they might be getting along better than they ever had, even before the divorce. Kelsey was enjoying her newfound freedom, and, because she wasn't using it to do anything dangerous or stupid, Stella was enjoying giving it to her. The only stipulation had been that Kelsey needed to keep her grades up, and even as much as she was going out lately, because she was so smart, they hadn't slipped.

Fortunately, even though she had a new boyfriend, Kelsey was spending her nights in groups. Stella didn't have a problem with that, provided that she texted her a photo of her friends together. She couldn't say that it didn't worry her to see her daughter coming home so late, but she was tolerating it, and the result was that her relationship with Kelsey was stronger than it had been in years.

"I think it needs something," Angela said, staring at the painting Stella had been working on for the past few days, the one she had tried to paint in her bedroom. It was sitting before them in the living room, still wrong, and Stella had brought it up to Angela for advice. "Or maybe it needs something taken away?"

Stella squinted, her gaze fixed on the work before her. It had been difficult to bring anything to Angela at first, particularly something so unfinished. She'd rarely painted with others, not to mention her idol, and she hadn't wanted for Angela to think this painting she was struggling so hard with was indicative of the best of her abilities. However, when Angela had shown her her own unfinished painting and asked for her advice, she'd learned that perhaps a bit of vulnerability could be a good thing. Looking at things from a different perspective had always been difficult for Stella, but she admired Angela and respected her input. She was one of the few people in the world who had a chance of changing Stella's mind on anything, these days. Divorce and hurt had made her stubborn.

"I agree," she said, "but I can't figure it out. I tried to challenge myself like you said, and it didn't do much but make a painting I don't love."

"Well, what was the challenge?"

Stella hesitated. "I painted in my bedroom instead of one of my studios." Angela laughed.

"Oh, honey. No. That's not really what I meant."

"Then what should I do?"

"Something crazy! Paint a photo, but turn it upside-down and try to paint it to look right. Close your eyes. Use one hand—better yet, use your teeth. Something that will change the way you look at your art."

Stella couldn't fathom the idea of painting with a paintbrush in her mouth, but she wasn't the expert here.

"You could try painting with someone watching," came Kelsey's voice from the kitchen doorway, startling Stella. "Sorry. I came in through the back door. I wanted to put my bike away."

"This is your daughter?" Angela asked, and Stella nodded.

"Yes. Angela, this is Kelsey. Kelsey, this is Angela Goff, the famous painter I've been telling you about." Kelsey shook her extended hand and smiled, greeting her politely.

"What's this about painting with someone watching?"

Kelsey shrugged, biting into the apple she'd snagged from the kitchen. "I don't know. I mean, I know my mom teaches classes, but that's different from painting something real. Whenever I take a test at school, I get really self-conscious when the professor is looking over my shoulder, but I tend to do better on the test because I'm double-checking my answers more. Mom's always shooed me out of the room when she's painting. Maybe painting with an audience might make you look harder at some of the details you normally wouldn't question."

Angela lit up, grinning. "That's brilliant," she said. "I think you should try it. We can do it tomorrow after you're finished teaching. I'll come by and watch you sketch out something." She turned back to Kelsey. "Are you following in your mother's artistic footsteps?"

She laughed. "Oh, definitely not. I'm not creative."

"That's not true," Stella interjected. "You're very creative and talented at everything you do. You've just never shown much of an interest in art, mine or anyone else's."

She nodded even as Angela's face fell with disappointment. "Art museums are, like, my least favorite type of museum. No offense. I'm sure your exhibits were lovely, but I'm just not built to understand things that are so abstract."

Angela shook her head. "That's a shame. You'd be good. In any case"—she turned to Stella—"you should start listening to your daughter more often."

Kelsey smirked. "Yeah, Mom. I agree."

"She's got some good ideas, and clearly, she means a lot to you. I think that anything you painted because of her would be a lot more meaningful. Not only that, but she went through the worst of everything with you. I mean, childbirth alone is enough trauma to last a woman a lifetime. When you add in the divorce and the move, you've got someone here who understands you better than anyone else could."

Stella considered that for a long moment. She wasn't wrong—Kelsey had gone through everything with her, and that was part of why she was so cautious about transferring any of those feelings into her work, particularly ones where her daughter was involved. She never wanted Kelsey to see the parts of her that were still hurt and angry and fearful that her past would catch up with her. She was meant to set a good example, and she wanted to show her that they could both move on from this.

"It is a good idea," she admitted, "the painting while someone watches. It makes me uncomfortable even just in the setting of class, when I'm painting things that are easy for me, so I think that someone watching over my shoulder as I tried to conceptualize an idea would definitely be enough to bring me out of my comfort zone, at the very least."

Kelsey looked to be a bit proud of herself as she bid the women goodnight and headed to her room.

"Teenagers are unpredictable, aren't they?" Angela asked. "One minute, you could swear they know absolutely nothing about the world, and the next, they show you shocking clarity."

Stella smiled. "Yeah, that pretty much sums it up. Do you have kids?"

Angela cackled. "Nope! I value my freedom far too much for that, sweetheart, I can tell you that. No, I worked with some interns a few years back, and a lot of them were fresh out of high school. They were a real treat, but kids aren't for me."

"Can I ask why not? You seem like you'd be great with them."

"Do I?" she asked. Stella shrugged, not knowing whether she'd just insulted her. It had been meant as a compliment, but perhaps it had read as judgmental. "I don't feel as though I'm the maternal type, to be frank with you. I'm far too selfish."

"Selfish? What do you mean?"

"Marriage, kids, dogs—they all tie you down. You lose some of your freedom when you promise your life to someone or something else."

Stella hadn't ever thought of Jeff or Kelsey as limiting to her dreams. Quite the opposite, in fact. She couldn't imagine her life without Kelsey, and for all his flaws, she had Jeff to thank for that. Though Angela wasn't saying it aloud, Stella could read between the lines. The "freedom" she was talking about wasn't just the ability to paint all night and go to sleep at 9:00 a.m. when inspiration struck because she didn't have any other mouths to feed. Nor was it about being able to drop everything and tour with an exhibit without having to worry about uprooting her child's life. What she was talking about was freedom of expression, the ability to say whatever she wanted with her art and not worry about the feelings of whoever she painted about. Angela could make whatever statements she wanted about her ex-husband because she wasn't co-parenting with him or relying on his mother for emotional support. If she thought he was the worst person in the world, she could say that about him.

Stella, on the other hand, didn't have such freedom. She had to think about the impact of her words on Kelsey.

If she hated Jeff, though she wasn't so sure anymore whether or not she really did, she couldn't say that, because he was the father of her daughter. It wasn't in Kelsey's best interests, no matter what he'd done, to hate her father. Everything Stella said about him she had to put through a filter, because she needed to ensure that Kelsey still knew how much he loved her. And that, in his own, incorrect way, he'd thought that he was doing something good for her. For better or worse, Angela didn't have to think about that. She was allowed to feel whatever emotions came up and didn't have to suppress them like Stella did.

Apparently Stella's silence was telling, because after a moment of quiet contemplation, Angela began to backpedal slightly. "Not that I'm trying to say you made the wrong choice or anything," she clarified, but her heart wasn't in it. "Just that it's a different lifestyle. You've got more at stake than I do. I'm sure that it's worth it for you, though. I can see how lovely your daughter is."

That didn't sit terribly well with Stella, the implication that her daughter was somehow detracting from her art career, but she wasn't going to argue with Angela. After all, it wasn't a terribly uncommon opinion for unmarried people without children to have, anyway. Felicia felt similarly, that she had more freedom to do what she liked because she'd never settled down. It was true, after all. Having a child did limit her in that way, but it was worth it. She wouldn't give it up for anything in the world. Still, she could see how someone who didn't have kids wouldn't understand that bond.

"No, I'm with you," she said. "Everybody picks the life

that they want, right? What's right for one person isn't necessarily right for another."

Angela's face fell in relief. "Exactly. I mean, everyone is always telling me I should have had children," she said, missing Stella's point entirely. "It's just not for me."

Stella tuned out the rant that followed, nodding politely while Angela changed the subject back to all the traveling she'd been able to do with her art, never outright bringing up the fact that it was something Stella likely could not do because of her daughter. She couldn't help but wonder what kind of art she might have created if she hadn't had to be conscious of someone else's feelings. Would it have been better? Was everything she painted fated to be dull because of the filter she had to put it through?

Chapter Three

The exhibit Stella thew with Angela was unlike any of the previous ones she had put together. She'd been proud of her two exhibits, and she still was, but the amount of professionalism that Angela was able to bring to the table was unbelievable. The catering had been from the fanciest local restaurants, as opposed to Stella's previous caterers who had been her restaurant-owner friends who had agreed to give her a deal if she patronized them for the event and advertised their food on her website. Sure, that had been wonderful for the locals, but the guests who had flown in from Europe at Graham's request during the second exhibit had been significantly less impressed. Angela was able to bring the best wines and cheeses, fresh breads, exotic fruits, and all kinds of fancy appetizers. Rather than having college students running around serving the guests, Angela had hired professionals, which Stella had to admit made a difference. They never let a wineglass go empty, never let someone walk around with trash in their hands for more than a second. Stella would have sworn that each of them had a sixth sense, but Angela reassured her that was just what a professional caterer looked like.

If she were being honest, it made her feel a bit out of her depth. The community here hadn't seen any artists in years—decades, even—and had been wildly impressed with what she'd been able to pull off. However, the people that had come to see Angela weren't nearly so easily swayed. By the end of the exhibit, Stella herself had felt more like an impressed visitor than a featured artist.

Her art had sold well, though. She'd worried that, next to Angela's, she wouldn't sell a single thing, that no one would even bother coming to look at her works when Angela's were on the opposite wall. But that hadn't been the case, not at all.

"This is a beautiful piece," one of Angela's friends, a tall man who was born in New York but had been living in Paris for the past five years, said. He spoke with a sort of put-on half accent, which made Stella want to roll her eyes. Angela had introduced her to a lot of people at the beginning of the event, so many that Stella couldn't keep track of them all, but this guy had stood out.

"Thank you," she said. He was eyeing one of her beachfront landscapes, something that she had a lot of on the wall. The one he was looking at had been painted at sunset, and the focal point was a local food truck that she loved. She hadn't expected that particular piece to appeal to anyone who wasn't from the area. "You can actually see the real thing out the window from here, or you could if it weren't so dark out."

"It's very pedestrian," he commented, "but not in a bad

Making Big Decisions

way. It makes me feel like I've been here before, like I live here." He smirked. "Not that I ever could—small-town life is not for me! I would simply die. But still, it's charming, in its own right."

Stella wasn't sure what she was supposed to make of that. A lot of Angela's friends spoke to her that way, with a sort of underlying condescension, but they were bidding on her works, so she couldn't complain. When he asked how much the painting was, Angela stepped in before she could say a word, immediately tossing him a price that was almost double what Stella herself would have asked for that piece.

"When your art is next to mine," she explained later, "you get to ask for more money for it. In fact, you have to. My own works won't sell as well if yours are so cheap, no offense."

Was this what fame did to artists, she wondered? Angela was so sweet and humble outside of this setting, but now, Stella was finding her a bit difficult to bear. Angela's attitude had shifted to match those of the buyers, which meant that she was acting snooty and haughty. She'd advised Stella to do the same, if not in so many words.

"You have to sell yourself," she'd said before the first guest arrived. "I know you're used to being the biggest fish in the smallest pond, but these are sharks, and they'll eat you alive if you don't bare some teeth. You might not like how you have to talk to them. I know I don't. But it's what you have to do to survive in this industry, and there's no better time than now to learn that."

Stella frowned. "How will I know what to say?" she asked. "I mean, I've been around rich crowds before, but never trying to sell my art. My husband's wealthy friends had always just treated my painting as a cute hobby. I've never had to take it this seriously before."

"I'll be right here," she promised. "If I hear you saying something wrong, I'll swoop in and save you."

"I can't ask you to do that all night."

Angela had laughed. "How do you think I learned? Someone more talented than I was at the time had to babysit me through my first big gallery. Even then, afterward, I made a million mistakes, and if you do, it's not the end of the world. I just don't want you to undersell yourself tonight. You can price your paintings however you want after this show, but for now, you're worth a fortune. You've got a name backing you, my name. I want you to be able to make the most of that and profit off it."

At the moment, Angela had managed to make that statement seem like she was doing it for Stella's benefit, but once she had seen it in practice, she'd become sure that it was only for her own. She was embarrassed to have her art hanging next to that of a nobody, even if she'd been the one to hunt down Stella and practically force her into a collaboration.

Speaking of the collaboration, that collection had sold almost immediately. Angela's pieces had sold faster, of course, but Stella's were right behind them. Angela had been right about her name attaching notoriety to her work. She'd never made so much off a single piece as she had for every canvas in their collection. Felicia had stopped by the gallery even though she was feeling slightly upset that she hadn't been chosen to cater this event. Kelsey and her new boyfriend Marco had even made an appearance, though

Making Big Decisions

Stella was fairly sure that Marco had requested the visit just to get on her good side.

"Stella," Angela said at the end of the night, forcing Stella's attention back to the moment. Her mind had been wandering to all the people she had talked to, wondering if she'd said the right things and rehashing conversations in her mind. "I can see smoke coming out of your ears. What are you thinking about?"

She forced a smile and shook her head. "Nothing," she lied. "Just taking it all in. It was a good night."

Angela might not have known her well, but Stella was easy to read, so she didn't buy her lie for a moment. "That it was," she said. "I was wondering if you'd like to join me for a drink."

Stella looked around the gallery, now empty but still extremely messy, and frowned. "I can't leave the gallery looking like this. I have classes to teach tomorrow."

"And you'll get to them!" she replied. "After a drink." With Angela, especially when she was either frustrated or celebrating, one drink was never just one drink. One glass of wine turned into a gin and tonic which turned into a Long Island iced tea, a taxi home, and a raging headache in the morning. Stella had seen her go through this cycle before, though not often, and had sworn that she wouldn't be a part of it. She wasn't Kelsey's age anymore. Still... she didn't have to drink as much as Angela did. She could stop at one glass of wine and get back to her gallery as soon as possible. Five years ago, if someone had asked her who she would want most in the world to have a drink with, she'd have said Angela Goff.

"One drink," she caved. "But I mean it, only one. I really have to get back here to clean up."

"I'll have you back before you know it."

Stella hesitated, but Kelsey, who stood nearby, rolled her eyes. "Go, Mom," she said. "Marco and I can clean."

"I'm not going to ask you to do that."

"You're not asking," Marco said. "We're offering." Stella could see that he didn't particularly love this plan, but he clearly liked Kelsey enough to tolerate it, so she smiled.

"Go out and let your hair down. Literally," she urged, gesturing to her tight updo that she'd styled for the evening. It was beginning to make her head ache, if she were being honest.

"All right," she reluctantly agreed. "But don't worry about the gallery. I'll be back before the end of the night and I'll put everything away. It's my mess, after all."

Kelsey waved her off and Stella led Angela to her car. She'd never actually been to a bar in town, and she was pretty sure that Angela wouldn't be impressed with a bar-and-grill restaurant, which was the closest she'd gotten. There would be one downtown, she assumed, so she put her keys into the ignition and drove in the vague direction of what she hoped would be the right destination.

Chapter Four

Several drinks later, Angela had not gotten Stella back to the gallery. By this time, she'd had not just a glass of wine, but two margaritas as well, something she hadn't drunk since college. They'd been strong, too, but for some reason, she hadn't felt the desire to stop after just one. The tequila was sharp against her tongue, but the salt around the rim made the entire drink go down quickly and easily. Before she knew it, she had already drunk one, then another, and now she was sitting at the bar feeling drunker than she'd been in a long time.

"You did great tonight," Angela slurred, and Stella couldn't help but flush, though whether that was the liquor or the embarrassment was anyone's guess. "I'm serious. You're a natural, talking to those art bigwigs. Some of them are real jerks, and you handled them perfectly."

Stella laughed. "I was a PTA mom," she explained. "I know how to handle passive aggression."

The biggest complaint that the other artists had expressed about Stella's art had been not with her paintings themselves, but with the subject. She painted landscapes, usually of the beach, and some of them found that to be safe, boring. Angela reached into the darkest recesses of her mind to pull out raw, dangerous art, whereas Stella was painting sunsets. She didn't agree with them, and clearly, neither did Angela, since she'd chosen her of all people to collaborate with, but it still hurt.

She tried not to let that sit with her for the remainder of the night, focusing instead on the fact that she was out with her idol and had just come from the most successful gallery showing she'd ever put together. She hadn't even heard the total of what she'd made tonight, but she knew it was outrageous just based on how many buyers she'd had. The only trade-off had been her class enrollment. Normally, during her galleries, her main source of income was the fact that people were signing up for her classes left and right. They all paid their down payments before class started so she could go buy them supplies, and she always came home with a list of names of eager students itching to start painting.

Tonight, however, she'd had no such luck. Her enrollment had been open, the sign for it clearly displayed in both the window and at the checkout desk, but hardly anyone had asked about it. She supposed that was probably mostly because of the fact that most of these new visitors were not locals, but people that Angela knew from the art world. They were either on or above Stella's level, so while they might have been impressed with her work, they certainly weren't looking to learn from her. In fact, she could probably take notes from each of them about all the things she didn't know about this strange new arena of her life. All she knew was painting. The rest, she was making up as she went along. She wondered how long faking it until she made it would hold out, or if she was going to crash and burn soon.

During their time drinking, Stella learned that Angela was actually a pretty normal person, when the art was stripped away and all she had to focus on was celebrating a victory. She laughed loudly and, with her head thrown back at all of Stella's jokes, made quips about people Stella had thought were Angela's friends. Apparently, Angela found a lot of them just as obnoxious as Stella had, even if she'd never say that to their faces. Stella could relate to that sentiment. It was how she had felt about a lot of Jeff's old friends, particularly those who were as rich as they had been when he'd been embezzling money. A lot of the time, she'd had to plaster a smile on her face and act like things were funny when she didn't think a joke had been very good, or pretend it didn't bother her when a grown man was rude to a waitress for being slow on a busy night in a restaurant. Jeff had always told her that he had to tolerate those people to get ahead in the world, and she'd never understood that sentiment. Why did he have to surround himself with people he didn't care for just to succeed?

Now, she was afraid that she was beginning to get it, and it wasn't a feeling she loved. However, with Angela close by to make fun of them with her, it didn't seem such an impossible task.

"You know," Angela began after several drinks. She was slurring her words and her eyes were tired, but Stella could tell that she was still lucid, just loose. "I wanted to ask you something."

Stella cracked a smile. "If I'll do an exhibit with you?" she tried. "Hate to say it, but we've been there, done that."

Her laugh was loud enough to be heard a table over, and Stella was sure that the couple sitting beside them had, indeed, heard it. She flashed them an apologetic wave.

"No," Angela said. She sat forward, a sobering intensity in her eyes. "I mean, yes, kind of. But not what you're saying. I mean I think we should open up a gallery together. Not just a one-night exhibit, but somewhere where our art can hang all in one spot. Everything you paint that you want to sell, some of my art that I haven't already promised to other people. We can even get other artists involved down the line, if we want to. What do you think?"

Stella chuckled. "I think you're drunk," she replied, feeling so herself. Angela would never in a million years be asking this of her if she were sober, would she? Sure, one exhibit had been fun and cute, but a whole gallery?

"I am drunk. But I'm also serious. I've been thinking about this a lot. It's not an impulse."

Stella couldn't help but roll her eyes. "You don't want to move your art here to Sunrise Beach. You would never be happy here." What Stella wanted to say was that Angela had done nothing but complain about how small the town was since she'd asked to do the exhibit, but she held her tongue, assuming that was probably better left unsaid. Angela was a big-city girl. Stella knew because she herself had become one after decades of living in Atlanta.

"Oh, definitely not. I'm not talking about moving here, Stella. I'm talking about you doing what you should do for your career. Anyway, if you're really serious about being an artist. We'd set it up in some art hub. Miami, Seattle, Baltimore, somewhere you can really get noticed by people who can advance your career. I noticed you by chance, but if you really want to do this, and I think you should, then you're going to have to make some changes, and one of the most important ones would be to move."

Stella shook her head. "I can't. I mean, we just settled down here."

"Then what better time would there be to move?" she asked. "Think about it. You have no family here, a yearly lease on the gallery you're currently renting. This place can't offer you much, but I can."

Stella wanted to say no, wanted to immediately tell her that she had no interest in moving, no interest in starting over. She'd done that once, and it had almost driven her crazy. Her life was constantly in motion, these days, and that wasn't what she'd ever wanted for herself. Part of why she'd gotten married so young had been the appeal of settling down, starting a life in one place. She'd always been a white-picket-fence kind of person. She hadn't even ever considered that there could be a different life for her.

Still, whether it was the alcohol or the undivided attention from one of her biggest idols, she found that the "no" didn't come from her lips, didn't even make it to her teeth. Stella couldn't shake her head in dissent or tell Angela that the life she was describing just wasn't her. Perhaps it was just because she was tipsy, or maybe it was because she'd done so well tonight in sales but not in art class sign-ups. But instead of telling her she wasn't interested, she put her chin in her hands and stared into her drink, thinking hard.

The thoughts were slow and muddled by the alcohol, probably just the way Angela had hoped they would be.

Though they hadn't known one another for long, Angela had probably figured out that Stella was a stubborn person at her core, and that the only way to get an idea through to her was to wait until she was vulnerable. The easiest way to induce that vulnerability had been to go out for drinks, and for a moment, she felt a little manipulated, but the earnestness in Angela's eyes dissolved that suspicion. No, this wasn't a ploy. It was an offer, and one that could, in fact, drastically change the course of her life if she agreed.

"Kelsey is in school," she said. "I can't be traveling all the time. She needs me here."

"She's a big girl," Angela argued. "By the time I was her age, I was living on my own in a tiny studio apartment, owing nothing to no one. I didn't have any help, and it made me a stronger person. Without that experience, I wouldn't have gotten as far as I did in life."

Stella's gaze hardened. "You can't possibly be suggesting that I kick my own daughter out of the house just so I can move to a completely different city and start over."

"I'd never ask you to do something you don't want to do. If you can't move right away, then we can work out a traveling position. You can work from here when you're painting, and when it's time to do events, we'll fly you out to the gallery. I know it'd be cumbersome, but it's just until Kelsey graduates or moves out of her own accord. I'm not pushing you to do anything."

"I don't know. I'd have to think about it when I'm not... you know, three drinks in."

She nodded. "I'm not looking for an answer right now. I just think that your mind and talents are really well suited to all of this! Not just the painting, but the rest of it, too.

Making Big Decisions

You threw exhibits all by yourself, with no one helping you, and both of them were, like, really good. Great, even. I mean, they got the attention of my talent scout, and he looks at seasoned professionals only. You should consider it a compliment that I'm suggesting this to you. I think you're good, and I don't want to see you squander it."

In more recent months, Stella had been struggling to think of herself more as a professional, career artist and less of a glorified hobbyist. She'd made a living off it for over a year now, enough to support both her and her daughter. It hadn't always been easy, and she certainly wouldn't have been able to do it without the introduction of the classes she was teaching, but it was a living doing what she loved. She would be lying if she said that the idea of making it big, of making even more money doing even less busywork and more of what she had set her sights on from the beginning—which was painting—wasn't appealing.

"I'll think about it," she promised, and she wasn't just saying it. Though she had no idea how it would work, the need to be in a different city than Sunrise Beach, she really did want to think about a way to make it work. After all, Kelsey had chosen the local community college because it was the only place cheap enough for them to afford. Maybe, if they had a little more money and were in a city with some better options, she would want to move. She had certainly complained enough about this place when they'd first moved here. Lately, she'd seemed happier, perhaps even happy. There was no way to tell how Kelsey might react to the idea of picking up and moving again.

It was getting late, and Stella was feeling a little nauseated from the alcohol. She hadn't realized she was drinking on a nearly empty stomach until now, but her nervous stomach had prevented her from having many appetizers at the event and now she felt pleasantly drunk, enough that it was probably time to call it a night. She called a cab and headed home, bidding Angela a good night and ensuring that she, too, was in a taxi on her way back to her hotel.

Chapter Five

When Stella got to bed that night, though the liquor had made her feel sleepy in the bar, she was now unable to fall asleep. Everything felt as though it were rocking, and she had to lay propped up by pillows, otherwise she could taste the drinks in her stomach. Keeping Stella awake more than the physical discomfort, though, was her racing mind. So much had happened tonight, even before Angela's proposal. She'd been noticed by one of her favorite artists, and because of that, a bunch of bigwigs who would normally never be interested in someone with so little notoriety had come and viewed her art, even purchased it. She was no longer just a painter in a community that hadn't seen an artist in decades. She was a professional.

She thought, not for the first time but certainly for the first time in a long while, about her old life. Not about Jeff, or Kelsey's old private high school, or any of the people she knew there, but her lifestyle. For what it was worth, she didn't often miss the lavishness of that life. Stella had never been a materialistic person, having grown up with very little, and that hadn't changed when Jeff had started bringing in an amount of money that had allowed them to buy whatever they wanted. Sure, she liked the vacations, the cruises, the big house, and the cleaning staff. It was fun to eat out at expensive restaurants that she wouldn't even be able to get into now.

Sending Kelsey to a private school had been a wonderful experience, and she'd been grateful for the things that his money had been able to do for her in her life—till it had all been taken away once he had been arrested and they'd lost it all. Regardless of what the FBI had confiscated, nothing could take away Kelsey's memories, nor her excellent education, nor the fact that she had grown up knowing that her parents could afford anything she wanted. They'd done their best not to spoil her, though Stella was aware that they often failed, but still, when she looked back on everything, she was happy about it.

No, it wasn't those lavish things that she missed, but the security. She had felt safe all the time. They'd always known that they could pay their bills. When Gwen, Jeff's mother, had needed shoulder surgery that her insurance refused to cover, they had been able to pay for that plus the months of physical therapy she'd needed afterward. They'd even been able to hire someone to help her upkeep her house and deliver her groceries when she'd been in too much pain to clean and hadn't wanted to leave the house. A car breaking down or an expensive house repair or any other unexpected hiccup that life tended to throw at them had never made her wonder if they would survive financially. She did miss that.

Last year, when someone had thrown a rock through the window of her gallery, she'd been nervous about paying for the repair. Her car, old and noisy, made her nervous almost every day, as she knew that if she needed to replace it for any reason, she wouldn't have a lot of options. Heaven forbid, if she needed to be hospitalized for any reason, that would break them. There existed worries that she hadn't needed to concern herself with when she was rich. Things she hadn't had to think about that now threatened, constantly, to overwhelm them without warning.

That was what she missed about having money. It wasn't the material possessions, but the security. The only thing she'd promised Kelsey when Jeff had gone to prison was that she would keep her safe, but there were a million things that she couldn't protect against. Some things, only money could buy, and for the past several years, there hadn't been much time where she hadn't been worried about their finances.

The next morning, Stella woke with a groan. Her head was pounding, her stomach felt poisonous, and she wanted nothing more than to drink an entire pot of coffee and crawl back into bed until at least noon. Unfortunately, she couldn't do that, as she'd made plans with Felicia for the morning to talk about how the exhibit had gone, and though she knew she could cancel, she really needed to talk to someone about it. Besides, there was caffeine in tea, right? She was sure she could get Felicia to hook her up with some kind of herbal hangover remedy that would kick her headache and nausea to the curb.

Felicia was waiting for her when Stella arrived, about ten minutes late, to their brunch. She had already had the kitchen prepare Stella's favorite breakfast sandwich (as Stella had forgotten to text ahead of time and tell her she was pretty sure that food would kill her), and a cup of her usual tea. When she saw Stella, her expression dropped from excited to concerned.

"You look ghastly!" she exclaimed, and Stella rolled her eyes.

"I don't look that bad," she defended, though she wasn't sure who she thought she was fooling. If she looked half as bad as she felt, then ghastly was an understatement. "I had too much to drink last night. Any suggestions?"

Felicia nodded. "Of course I have suggestions. Oh, dear, you should have told me beforehand." She called one of the girls over and ordered Stella a cup of green tea with ginger and honey. Normally, Stella would turn her nose up at something like that, but if it would help, she was willing to try anything. "Dare I ask how the event went?"

"Oh, the event was amazing. It was the partying afterward that was ill-advised."

Felicia laughed softly, watching as Stella massaged her temples with her fingers. "Poor thing. I don't pity you too much, you know. You did this to yourself. How much did you drink last night?"

Stella tried to recall and failed. It wasn't like she'd gotten carried away with some kind of wild and crazy night, but she so rarely drank anything but a glass of wine here and there, and on an empty stomach, it had wrecked her. "Too much," she replied. "I don't even want to think about how Angela is doing right now. Honestly, I should text her just to make sure she's still alive. I haven't heard from her this morning."

"I'm sure she's sleeping. She took you out afterward? I'm guessing it was a celebration, or were you drowning sorrows?"

Stella shook her head. "The exhibit was amazing. I sold my art for more than I've ever made in my life. All the pieces were sold before it was even halfway over, and to real art collectors, too. Like, European guys with hundreds of thousands of dollars that they pour into these collections. It was amazing. I couldn't even believe how many connections she has."

"So, if it went so well, why do you look like someone spat in your cereal this morning?"

Stella hesitated. As much as she felt she needed to get last night's conversation off her chest, now, in the clarity of sobriety, she wasn't sure if it was even going to be an issue. Perhaps Angela had just been drunk and suggested an idea that she would rescind today. She may or may not have been serious, and even if she were, Stella had no way of knowing if her conviction was going to be quite as strong as it had been last night. Honestly, it probably wouldn't be, and she wasn't sure whether that made her feel better or worse about the whole thing. Did she want the offer to be real?

"Well, she sort of ran a proposal by me last night. Opening an art gallery in a big city, where we'd sell our art together just like we did last night. We could collaborate more, too. She was drunk when she pitched it, but she swore that she'd been thinking about it for a while."

Felicia was surprisingly quiet. Stella felt the need to say

more, but she didn't know what she would fill the silence with. It wasn't as if she needed to justify herself to Felicia, and besides, she wasn't even sure if she was really thinking about the offer in any serious capacity.

"That's quite a conversation," Felicia finally said, cryptic in a way she so rarely was. Felicia always spoke her mind and never hesitated to let people know how she felt. "What did you say to her?"

Stella shrugged. "Nothing, really. I was drinking, too. I told her I'd have to think about it."

That answer didn't seem to please Felicia, though she didn't seem upset, either. For the first time that Stella had ever seen, she was demonstrating a poker face, and it was frustrating.

"And have you thought about it? Do you know what you want to say?"

"I think you have an opinion on what I should say."

She sighed. "Stella, I think your art is wonderful, and I believe in you wholeheartedly. I have no doubts that if you moved back to the big city, that you could thrive there just like you have here."

"But..."

"But," she finished, "I think you've worked your tail off to get where you are today. After everything with your ex, I know things were nearly impossible. You told me what dark days those were, how difficult it was to see the light at the end of the tunnel. You mentioned a similar feeling when you moved to Atlanta for the first time. I don't want you to have to go through that all over again in a new city. It's so hard to put down roots and have to keep pulling them up, don't you think?"

Stella considered this. Sure, she might have more room for advancement in a big city, but it would also mean more competition, not to mention that she would have to start all over. She'd only gotten as far as she had in Sunrise Beach because of her determination, but it had taken a lot of time. She was the only artist who had lived here in years. How was she going to make a name for herself somewhere populated by other artists, even if Angela were willing to help her? Starting over would mean giving up everything she had worked for here, which had only just begun to pay off. After putting her entire heart into this for so long, was she really willing to give it up so easily just for the possibility of something better?

"You're right," she finally agreed. "That's certainly something to consider."

Stella felt torn. On the one hand, she missed big-city life. She missed the hustle and bustle of it all, the fact that there were always a million opportunities to do anything she was interested in, and the endless inspiration for her art. However, she was just beginning to feel at home here, and that was something she wasn't sure she was ready to give up. Everyone in Sunrise Beach was so kind, and had been from the very beginning. If she left, she would miss them all terribly, so much that she wasn't sure she could bear it. Leaving her so-called friends in Atlanta had been an easy decision. In fact, they and their gossip were a large part of the reason she decided to move at all. Moving away from here would be a different story entirely. It would feel like moving away from home.

Of course, there were always times when leaving the familiar comforts of home was necessary to grow and develop. Was this one of those times? Was the universe telling her to stay, or to go?

Chapter Six

When Kelsey returned home that afternoon, she was beaming, a mood that Stella had not seen her wear in a long time. Normally, she walked through the door texting or on the phone, mumbled a brief hello to her mother, denied wanting a healthy snack or lunch as she dove into the pantry for a bag of chips, and headed straight to her room to study or watch *Grey's Anatomy*. Stella had even tried to watch the show just to have a talking point with her, but there were so many seasons and Stella had given up quickly. She'd never catch up with her, so she resigned herself to just assuming that another dreamy doctor had left the show every time Kelsey came into the kitchen in the evening, weepy-eyed and furious, for hot chocolate.

"You're in a good mood," Stella remarked as Kelsey sat down at the table, something she never did. "Good day at school?" Kelsey nodded.

"It was, actually." She didn't leave, almost looking like she might want to talk more about her day. Stella tried not to let her excitement show.

"Do you want a snack? I could make you a sandwich or something."

Kelsey smiled. "That sounds good, Mom. Thanks."

Stella turned away from her to grab sliced turkey, Swiss cheese, and lettuce from the refrigerator, biting her lip to keep from smiling.

"So, how was your day?" she asked casually.

"Well, you know how we started the new semester of classes a few weeks ago..." Stella hummed in affirmation. "Well, we just had our first test in my microbiology lab, and I did really well."

"That's wonderful, honey. Congratulations." Stella failed to see why this was so exciting—Kelsey had been bringing home nearly straight A's since she started kindergarten.

"I really love this class. I think it might be my favorite subject. And the professor is so cool. She's a research scientist, and this is the only class she teaches. She doesn't teach the actual class, it's just the lab that's like three hours a week. But that's the part I really love. When she handed back the test, she asked me to stay after class for a little bit."

Stella frowned. "Oh, no. What happened?"

Kelsey laughed. "Right? That's what I thought. I was, like, freaking out. Turns out, though, I wasn't in trouble. She said that there's an opening in her research lab, and she was looking to fill it. She wants a student."

"Oh, Kelsey, a job? I thought we'd talked about this. I don't want you to have to worry about this during the school year. You can work over the summers if you want." She'd have her whole life for working, Stella thought. She wanted to protect what were supposed to be the best years of her life. She was supposed to be having fun.

"It's not a job. It's an internship. Since she wants a student, she's willing to be flexible with my schedule."

Stella considered this. An internship might not be a bad idea, especially now that Kelsey wasn't going to the Ivy League school they'd always planned for her. It would get her foot in the door in terms of experience in the field she was so excited about, not to mention all the networking possibilities. It was always good to know people, and Kelsey was old enough to decide if this was something she wanted to pour her time into. And if it kept her a little more focused on school and a little less focused on her new boyfriend, Stella wasn't going to complain about that, either. She set the sandwich on the table in front of Kelsey, who took it with vigor.

"Well, if that's something you want to apply for, I say go for it. It's fantastic that she invited you, and it'd be a great opportunity to see if this is something you like enough to want to consider it as a career path."

Kelsey nodded. "I thought so, too! I mean, I always thought I'd get a master's degree, or maybe even a PhD, so I really want to spend time in the lab to see if I'm any good at it."

Stella rolled her eyes. "I'm sure you'll be amazing," she said. "I just don't want it to take away from your study time, or your time to hang out with your friends. Everyone needs time off. I want to make sure you're taking care of yourself."

"It's only sixteen hours a week," she said. "It'd be after class for a few hours during the week. The lab doesn't operate on weekends, so I'd still have plenty of time off, and as long as I'm keeping up with studying, that shouldn't be an issue, either. I really want to do this."

"Then I wish you luck. If there's anything you need, recommendation letters or anything, just let me know."

Kelsey smiled. "She wants a resumé. Can you show me how to make one?"

For the remainder of the afternoon, Kelsey was in a remarkably good mood, clearly both excited for the opportunity and proud of herself for having earned it. It made Stella wonder how she could even consider moving away again. It had taken so long for them to get adjusted here, and Kesley had only just gotten her bearings. There was no way she could take that away from her, and it was obvious, as Stella walked her through how to create her first resumé, that she was nowhere near ready to be left on her own. Unless she wanted to travel, which she was sure would exhaust her, she was going to have to tell Angela that she wasn't interested in the offer.

Sometimes, when Stella wanted to hear a certain answer, she asked the person whom she knew would provide her with that advice. She'd made the mistake of first taking this problem first to Felicia, who she knew would try to convince her to stay. It had been a good idea to hear her friend's perspective, of course, but it hadn't been what she'd really wanted. Because of that, she was pretty sure that she'd only taken it slightly to heart. The rest, she had chalked up to Felicia not being an artist, not understanding the dilemma that she was in.

Rather than dwell on this by herself or asking any of her friends in this tiny town, she called her mother-in-law, Gwen. This was something she still did at least once a week, though at one point in her life, for many years, they'd talked once a day. Gwen was like a mother to Stella, and she trusted her completely.

"It sounds like an amazing opportunity," Gwen said when Stella finished explaining. "What's keeping you from accepting?"

Stella sighed. "A million things," she admitted. "First, I already have my feet on the ground here. I have my gallery and my classes, which are going well."

"But you said that you didn't get as many sign-ups for that as you usually do, right?"

"Well, yes, but—"

"It's dangerous to put all your eggs in the same basket, dear. You can't possibly sell paintings in this little town forever, can you?"

"No, I can't. I know that. I sometimes feel like I'm working against a clock, like eventually I'll run out of people to sell my paintings to and people who want to buy my art and I'll have nothing left."

Gwen chuckled. "I'm not sure it'll be that dramatic, dear," she said, "but it's not a bad idea to think about it. You loved Atlanta, didn't you? You always used to tell me how much more lively this city was than your hometown."

That was true, of course, but Stella had been a teenager back then. She'd grown up in a town so small that she and her friends had to drive for hours on a weekend just to get to the nearest mall, so when she'd moved to Atlanta, where there was a shopping center or movie theater or arcade on every corner, she had been thrilled. That had become slightly less important to her as she'd grown, but it didn't mean that she didn't sometimes miss the big city. She did, often.

"It's true, but I've found a lot of charm in this small town, too. I loved the big city, but I love it here, too."

Gwen sighed. "I just want you to be happy, honey. With all you've been through, you deserve that very much. I just don't want you to settle, you know?"

Was that what she was doing, settling? Was it really so wrong to want a big life in a small town?

"I'll think about it," she agreed. "I don't know what to do just yet. I need to think about what's best for Kelsey, too."

"Of course. I know you'll make the right choice."

Stella poured herself a glass of wine after the phone call and sat on the couch, putting on a mindless reality television program in the background. Though she was hoping it would be dramatic enough to distract her, she found her thoughts consistently migrating back to the choice ahead of her. To quiet the noise, she took a long sip of wine and leaned her head against the back of the couch, closing her eyes while the lull of the television pulled her into sleep.

Chapter Seven

Stella woke on the sofa the next morning, her back and neck sore from having spent the night on the couch. She'd been so busy lately that her sleep had been neglected, and she supposed she had just finally crashed. Before she could wonder what had woken her, the sound came again, a pounding on the door. She stood, stretching her back with a groan as she did so, and peered through the peephole of the door.

Outside stood Angela Goff, up earlier in the morning than she had ever seen her. She opened the door despite the fact that she was still in her pajamas and hadn't yet brushed her teeth.

"Angela?" she asked. "What are you doing here?"

"Don't be mad at me," she said, and Stella groaned.

"Are you going to give me a reason to be mad at you?"

"Well... I hope not. I want to invite you to Seattle with me."

"What?" It was too early in the morning for this. "When? And what are we going to do there?"

"It's where I think we should open this gallery. I want to show you around the city. It's not fair to ask you to seriously think about moving somewhere you've never seen, and I know that. So, the solution is that we go visit Seattle, right?"

Stella hesitated. "I can't. Kelsey—"

"Is taken care of. I spoke with Felicia, and she said that she would check in on Kelsey every day and make sure she's taken care of. Kelsey said that she would stay with her friend Mariah for the week. Mariah's parents are fine with it. There's no reason to say no, so please say yes."

Stella's mind was reeling. She couldn't just leave, could she? She'd traveled before, but it was never the most relaxing experience in the world, and certainly nothing that she could begin at the last minute. It took weeks of planning, and even then, she always felt like she was forgetting something by the end of it.

"I can't just up and leave, Angela. I would need to pack."

"No need!" she chirped. "Everything is taken care of. I have a wardrobe lined up for you, food is paid for, and all you could need in toiletries are included in our hotel arrangement. I've got my personal assistants running around to get things ready. The only thing you need is a carry-on for the plane."

"You should go, Mom," came Kelsey's voice from behind her. She whirled around to find her standing in the living room, phone in hand. "Mariah's parents already agreed to let me sleep over for the week, and there's, like, nothing going on at school right now. I won't be alone with Marco, either, since Mariah's parents are strict about boys coming

Making Big Decisions

over. You can even keep in touch with her parents to make sure I'm there every night."

Kelsey was being uncharacteristically supportive, even going so far as to deny herself what could be a week to be free to visit her boyfriend without parental supervision. Of course, she knew what Stella would be concerned about. She must have really wanted her to go on this trip if she was promising to not see Marco in the evenings for a week.

"It's just so sudden."

"It's spontaneous. You need to do more of that. Your art will only be better for it."

"Mom, I know you like to be organized and everything, but just look at what happened to us in the past few years. When things were all up in the air and we had no idea what was going to happen, you were unshakeable. Every night, you promised me that everything was going to be all right, and it was. And now, we're doing better than ever!" The fact that Kelsey believed that was news to Stella, and it could have brought a tear to her eye if she weren't so stunned.

"Just say yes," said Angela. "We have to leave for the airport in half an hour, if you want to go with me. I'm sorry to spring this on you, but I need an answer, and I knew that if I didn't twist your arm, you'd never say yes."

Stella took a steadying breath, trying to sort through her racing thoughts. There were pros and cons to both choices, but she didn't have time to weigh them. It was true that she probably wouldn't have agreed to this if she weren't put on the spot, but with a plane waiting, a daughter with plans to stay with her friend already, and her idol standing before her flashing her pleading eyes, she didn't have another choice.

"Give me twenty minutes to pack my carry-on bag."

As she ushered Angela inside to wait on the couch and turned to her own bedroom, Stella couldn't help but feel her heart rate begin to speed up in either nervousness, excitement, or some combination of the two. This wasn't her. Stella wasn't the type of woman who left on spontaneous trips, especially ones that were meant to further her artistic career. She had no idea what Angela was going to show her on this trip, but Seattle was one of the few places that she'd never traveled to. Jeff didn't like the rain, nor was he a fan of coffee or heights. The thought of seeing the Space Needle made him sweat, but it was always somewhere she'd been interested in just because of the art culture in Washington. Not to mention, she'd painted so many beaches, but rarely got to visit National Parks and forests. She was looking forward to having a new landscape to inspire her.

Quickly, Stella shoved things into a bag—her headphones, her phone charger, her laptop. Cursing under her breath at the limited timespan, she tried not to feel too much anxiety over what she was missing. After all, Angela's assistants could help her get almost everything she could possibly need in Seattle.

"Stella! Hurry up, the plane is going to take off without us!"

Knowing she had no more time, Stella decided that she had packed as well as she could, so she zipped up her bag and headed down the hall to meet Angela, who ushered her out the door and to the taxi that was parked outside and waiting to take the two of them to the airport.

Of course, Angela was able to pay the extra money for a nonstop flight, but it still took over six hours to get from her home in North Carolina to Seattle-Tacoma International Airport. Angela had sprung for them to fly first class, a taste of a lifestyle that Stella had not known in years. By the time the plane landed, she was eager to stretch her legs.

She forced herself through baggage claim, something she had always hated doing, and when the two of them finally had their luggage, Angela led her to the taxi that was waiting to take them to their hotel.

"Wait till you see this place," Angela started. "It's right in the heart of the city. It actually overlooks one of the places I was considering looking into renting for the gallery, if you choose to do it. I'll point it out to you." Stella bit down on a smile. She'd known that this trip was designed to sell her on the gallery, but she hadn't expected that the convincing would start so soon.

"I'm starving," she said. "What do you say we find somewhere to eat after we put our things down in the hotel? I'm sure they have room service."

"Nonsense! Room service is for the unadventurous. You and I are going out to find somewhere good to eat, and I'm not taking no for an answer. We'll explore the city for a while."

Stella was tired, but she knew that she couldn't argue.

On top of that, she was curious, and she certainly didn't want to spend the whole trip in the hotel room.

"That's a good idea. I have to change, first."

The taxi dropped them off in front of the hotel, where a young bellboy came to grab their luggage out of the trunk and load it onto a cart. Angela told him their room number so he could get a head start while she retrieved the room key from the front desk, and she handed one to Stella and pocketed the other.

By the time they got to their room, their luggage had beat them there. Stella had only brought her single carry-on bag, though Angela herself had packed much more reasonably for a week-long trip. But Angela had promised to take care of everything, and it didn't take long for Stella to see that she had, indeed, done that. Angela had filled the closet with a full wardrobe of clothes, save for the undergarments that she'd had Stella bring herself.

"Angela," she breathed as she looked into the closet, "you didn't have to do this." It was only a few outfits, but they were all much sleeker and more stylish than Stella normally dressed these days. They reminded her of the clothes she'd worn in Atlanta, where she was always trying to impress Jeff's friends.

"I want you to really be able to envision the life you'll be living here, Stella. Everything from the clothes you'll wear to the coffee shop you'll get your latte from in the mornings. We're going to see everything the city has to offer, and only then can I ask you to make your decision about whether you want to make a business here."

Stella sighed. "Okay. I can't guarantee that I'll say yes

Making Big Decisions

even if you show me a really good time, but I'm willing to keep an open mind."

Angela seemed satisfied with that. After Stella showered the stale feeling of a long plane ride off her skin and changed into a pretty black blouse and a pair of bright red slacks that Angela had bought her, they were ready to leave the hotel and find a place to get lunch.

Angela took Stella to a deli with one of the best Reuben sandwiches she'd ever had. From there, they walked a few blocks down the road and toured an art museum, one that Stella had always wanted to visit. Angela's own work had been displayed here when she had toured years ago, though now that room was filled with the art of a refugee woman who came to America with only the ability to make intricate and beautiful pottery, which she used to make enough money to send for her sister. Both of them had been able to become citizens because of the financial stability her art had provided, and now a lot of her pottery was on display here because her story had been so inspiring and her art was beautiful.

"Art really is powerful, isn't it?" Stella asked as they stared at the exhibit, and Angela nodded.

"It saves lives. I know it saved mine, and I think you feel similarly. I would have lost my mind after my divorce had I not been able to paint."

"Honestly, I still can't believe just how fortunate I've been. I didn't know what I was going to do to provide for Kelsey after the IRS took everything. I had thought I was going to have to get a job as a receptionist or something, which would have been miserable. I would have done it, of course, but I wasn't looking forward to it. When my friend gave me the opportunity to set up the gallery, I only gave myself a few months to prove myself before I was going to give up and get a different job. I got lucky."

"No, you didn't. You're talented, and people recognize that in you. It's not luck. It was a matter of time before someone saw something amazing in you. I'm just happy that it was me, because I'm so excited about what we could create together."

Though Stella wasn't entirely sure that Angela wasn't just trying to butter her up a bit, it was flattering to hear from someone she had admired for so long. The fact that Angela wanted to work with her at all still felt like a dream, and it was one she hoped she didn't wake up from anytime soon.

That night, Stella collapsed onto her hotel bed without even changing out of her clothes. Angela laughed.

"Tired?"

"Jet lag," she admitted. "I think I'm going to get some sleep, if that's okay with you."

"Of course. I'm beat, too. We can start again tomorrow morning. I've got a great little café picked out, and after that, there are some people I want you to meet. If you want to take a look at those travel brochures that the hotel gave us, we'll go anywhere you want, as well."

Though she wasn't sure that she could keep her eyes open for long enough to do that, Stella agreed. "I want to check out the National Park. I would really like to paint there, I think."

Making Big Decisions

Angela bid her goodnight and left her room through the connected suite door, leaving Stella alone on her bed. Reluctantly, she hauled herself up and changed into the pajamas that Angela's assistants had provided for her, brushed her teeth, and snuggled back under the covers, too tired to even turn on her alarm.

As it turned out, she didn't need an alarm set on her phone because Angela had ordered her a wake-up call at 6:30 in the morning. Stella groaned as she reached for the phone, feeling as if she'd only just fallen asleep, before thanking the front desk employee and rolling back over to get a few more minutes of shut-eye. Unfortunately, she wasn't able to sleep for long before Angela was knocking on her door.

"Be ready to go in twenty minutes," she called. It brought back memories of all the family trips they had taken when Kelsey was a teenager and wanted nothing more than to sleep until noon no matter where they were, and Stella had been the one to have to get her up early every morning for sightseeing. Now, she understood Kelsey's pain and why she'd always insisted on being left behind until lunch, but since this was an all-expenses-paid trip to somewhere she'd always wanted to visit, she pulled herself out of bed and took a cold shower to wake herself up.

Nineteen minutes later, she stood in front of Angela wearing an emerald pantsuit and a silver necklace. First things first, they sought out coffee, which they got from a little café near the hotel. After a cup, Stella began to feel more like herself, and she was able to look at their itinerary with excitement for the first time. They started with another museum, one filled with classic paintings rather than the one they'd viewed yesterday that had been mostly modern pieces. They spent hours combing the whole museum, and when they finished, Angela took her for lunch at an authentic Chinese restaurant that served the most delicious hand-pulled noodles Stella had ever had.

Two more days passed like that, with Angela planning out their every minute. She took Stella to cafés, fancy restaurants, and all kinds of attractions around the city, not just the museums.

"You need to get a taste of everything there is to do around here," she'd explained. "Kelsey would love it, too." Just to appeal to Stella's softest spot, she even took her to the places that Kelsey, a lover of science, might enjoy, including the natural history museum, the botanical gardens, and an aquarium.

Chapter Eight

By the start of the sixth day of their trip, Stella had no idea how they were going to fill another four. She'd already met marketing executives who taught her the basics of selling her art and, more importantly, selling herself to prospective buyers. Much of it consisted of tactics she'd already been using unconsciously, but hearing it in such black and white terms was as helpful as it was off-putting. Her creative side didn't like to think of people who admired her art as potential customers and the target of her sales tactics. But she understood it was necessary to her success. When she added her own flair it was easier. Angela had praised her, saying that she was a natural. In addition to that, Stella had met artists, museum curators, and auctioneers, all of whom Angela had promised would help her build her career, if she let them.

"I have someone I want you to meet," Angela explained over coffee that morning. She'd already introduced Stella to several artists around town, all of whom had been nothing but sweet to her. None of them were anything like the pretentious people Angela had invited to the exhibit. These people were down to earth, humble, even. Stella had liked them a lot, and could have seen herself becoming friends with them, something she had to admit intrigued her. The idea of having a group of artist friends, rather than just her students and the occasional art-loving stranger, was something she lacked as of now.

"Oh? Who would that be?"

"Well, I've introduced you to some of the friendlier artists I like to collaborate with, but now, it's time to show you the other side of this business. You're going to meet with one of my marketing directors, David. You have to learn how to handle these guys."

Stella found the way she spoke of this man a little odd. Could he really be so bad?

"I'll just follow your lead."

Angela took Stella to a bistro to meet with David, who was already sitting in a small booth that didn't look big enough for two people, in Stella's opinion. Stella herself was rather thin from jogging every day, but Angela had a bigger bone structure, and David was a much larger man. Angela pulled up a chair and allowed Stella to sit across from David while she took the third spot.

"Hey, you!" Angela exclaimed, feigning an excitement to see him that Stella would not have anticipated, given the warning she'd been given. "It's been too long."

"It has. How have you been? I've heard you've been traveling the country."

She rolled her eyes. "When am I not?" He chuckled. "David, this is my good friend Stella. She's an artist, too. We actually just put an exhibit together. She's incredibly talented, and our collaboration was one of the best pieces I've created in a long time. I'm showing her around the city because I want her to move here and get her career started for real."

Stella reached out and shook his hand, surprised by the earnest introduction. "It's nice to meet you. I've heard good things."

At that, he scoffed. "Well, at least I know she's a convincing liar," he said to Angela. "She needs me more than she'll admit, and I don't bite as hard as she'd have you believe."

Angela called the waiter over and the three of them ordered, then she turned to David. "All right, there's plenty of time for small talk after we get down to business. I was wondering how you're doing on getting me another spot in the SAM." Angela scanned Stella's face for signs of confusion, but she was keeping up so far. She knew that the Seattle Art Museum had been one of the first big breaks that Angela had ever gotten. It was probably sentimental to her, Stella thought. That would explain why she seemed so eager to get in once more.

David sighed. "Look, just like I've told you, unless you're a long-dead famous person, the SAM isn't into repeat performances. They displayed your art once, so you're a bit of a hard sell. They want to know what makes your art so different now that it'd be worth another display."

"All new pieces, for starters," Angela huffed. "My exhibit was popular. Shouldn't that be enough?"

"It's the Seattle Art Museum, Angie." Stella watched her wince at the nickname she'd told Stella before that she hated. "They made you famous, not the other way around."

"I know that. Still, try them again. Who else are they looking at for the open spot?"

David shrugged, but under a glare, finally caved. "Vidhan Chakravarti. He's an Indian immigrant raising a deaf daughter alone because his wife passed away from cancer. He paints with her to stimulate her visually, since she can't hear. It's a pretty heartwarming story that went viral on the internet a few months ago, and they're looking to give him and his kid a whole exhibit."

Though the story was enough to bring Stella to tears, Angela looked annoyed. "Everyone's got a sob story," she dismissed irritably. She turned to Stella as if expecting her to agree. "The internet is ruining everything for us real artists, don't you think? We dedicate years of our lives to learning the craft, then someone who finger paints with his kid is suddenly a professional artist. It's honestly incredible."

Stella felt at a loss for words. She certainly didn't agree. Art was, at its core, a way to express oneself, and what could possibly be more artistic than using painting to connect two hearts who were struggling to communicate? Of course, it wasn't the same as learning techniques and spending hours painting and repainting the same scene trying to get it just right, but that didn't mean that it wasn't art. In fact, it was probably more beautiful than anything Angela could ever hope to paint. However, she didn't want to start an argument in front of David, and Angela didn't appear to be looking for a response, anyway. When Stella remained silent, she steamrolled ahead, turning her attention once more to the exhibit.

"Like it or not, he's what's hot right now. People want to come see his work."

"So, what I'm hearing is that I need to work on my public image, play up the things that made me start painting in the first place. If I get a following going on the internet, do you think I could have a chance at the spot?"

"I make no promises, but it certainly couldn't hurt. I'll do what I can on my end with marketing, and I'll let you know what I need from you."

The ease with which Angela accepted this and changed the subject to lighthearted chatter about the sightseeing they had done so far in Seattle was unnerving to Stella. She'd been appalled the entire time Angela had been speaking, frankly, and had expected at the very least for that to be something that Angela acknowledged as wrong. The SAM exhibit had been what had launched Angela's career. It had taken her from being a struggling divorcee without so much as a penny to her name to a thriving household name in the art world, and yet she still was willing to shove what sounded like a deserving candidate for the open spot out of the way to get what she wanted. This was a new side to Angela, one she hadn't known existed, and she wasn't a fan of it.

Stella struggled to smile through the remainder of the lunch. She laughed when Angela did, though her mind was so far elsewhere that she usually hadn't even registered a joke, and even if she had, she wasn't in a jovial mood. Her appetite was ruined and she barely managed to pick at the meal she'd ordered, instead opting to move it around her plate so it looked like she was taking bites. When asked a question, she replied, but other than that, she remained relatively quiet. She hoped that Angela wouldn't notice, but if she were being completely honest with herself, she wasn't sure she cared. Surely, Angela knew already that what she was doing was wrong. Stella had to tell herself this was a decision that was motivated by nostalgia and a personal loyalty to the museum, and not a reflection on Angela's character.

Still, when she thought of that man and his deaf daughter finger painting together, her little face lighting up with a connection with her father she'd never experienced before and couldn't have without the wonder of art, she couldn't shake the sick feeling in her stomach about Angela brushing it off as a "sob story" similar to her own. Stella herself was no stranger to tragedy, but she knew in her heart just how fortunate she really was. Though her parents had passed when she was young and she had had to live with all the horrors of the past four years since Jeff's arrest, she had her health, and more importantly than that, she had a daughter who had no obstacles standing between her and her dreams. She couldn't imagine how devastated she would be if she had to watch Kelsey struggle from a young age.

David asked Stella a few questions about her art, but she could tell that he wasn't particularly interested. He wasn't taking on new clients. Angela had told her that from the start, and, of course, she wasn't looking for a marketing manager despite how much Angela swore she needed one. Stella liked the website she had made with her students. It was a reflection of herself and her art style, and she wasn't

Making Big Decisions

looking to become famous on the internet for anything. On the contrary, that might have been her worst nightmare. She didn't need her name circulating again, not when Jeff's would only be a single click away.

When David excused himself for the afternoon, he didn't even offer to pay, expecting Angela to take care of it, which she did without complaint. Stella really didn't understand their relationship.

"So," Angela started as she fished for her wallet in her massive purse, "what did you think?"

"Of David? He was nice."

"No, not of him. I mean, not him specifically. I meant the entire interaction. You could use someone working for you, Stella, someone who can get your name out there. Every successful artist needs a David."

Stella wasn't sure that she could ever entrust her beloved marketing plan to someone else, but she nodded, anyway. "I suppose I could think about it," she said, though she was relatively certain her mind was made up already. "I was wondering, Angela. You're not really going to try to beat out that poor father and his disabled daughter for a spot in the SAM, are you?"

Angela looked at her like she had grown a second head. "Of course I am," she said. "What you'll learn, Stella, is that people who aren't broken in any way shape or form don't get into art, or at the very least, they don't get beyond sketching fruit in a bowl. Everyone you will meet here will tell you a sad story. Half of them aren't even true, or at least are an enormous exaggeration of the truth."

"So you don't believe him?"

"I'm not saying that. I'm saying that it doesn't matter.

What matters is talent, making good products. Artists like us who rely on our notoriety for survival need the exposure more than Vidhan. Do you even know how wealthy his family is in India? They're loaded, and they send him money all the time."

"How do you know that?"

She shrugged. "I've got spies on the inside, I suppose. I'll keep it at that."

Honestly, Stella was beginning to feel uncomfortable. What Angela was showing her about the necessary sacrifices that had to be made to get anywhere in this business weren't things she was sure she could accept. How could she do what Angela just did, send an assistant in to try to procure a spot that could go to someone who clearly deserved it? Would she ever be that tough, and did she even want to be?

Chapter Nine

Stella wasn't able to hide the fact that she was beginning to feel a bit weird about this whole trip. Seeing that side of Angela had been uncomfortable, and she wasn't sure what she was thinking about having her as her mentor anymore. On the one hand, she was one of Stella's favorite artists. She looked up to her immensely, and she knew that Angela could skyrocket her career to heights she could never have imagined, heights she couldn't reach on her own.

On the other hand, though, she had her own moral code she needed to stick to. There were things she wasn't willing to compromise on, and although Angela hadn't technically done anything wrong, Stella hadn't slept well thinking about it. She tried to let it go and shove it from her mind. Perhaps she was overreacting. After all, Angela had had a point, even if she didn't agree, about art galleries being reserved for those who had done the work to study the craft, those who relied on the income. Stella could understand that. Angela must know a lot of starving artists, far more than Stella did. Even Angela's own income was reliant on her popularity, though she was in no way struggling to make ends meet. Maybe it was a matter of principle and Stella was just being overly sensitive because the man's story had pulled at her heartstrings. She would be the first to admit that she could sometimes be blinded by her emotions and struggle to see the bigger picture.

When she woke the next morning, still groggy from her night of tossing and turning, she was determined to put the previous day behind her and start anew. She dressed herself in a sweater, scarf, and corduroy pants and headed down to the lobby to meet Angela, who frowned slightly upon seeing her.

"For someone who went to bed at seven, you don't look like you slept at all," she said. "How are you feeling?" Stella hadn't felt like spending the evening in a bar with Angela, so she had said that her stomach was feeling off and went back to her room early. It hadn't been a lie, exactly, but she'd allowed her to believe that the churning was something she ate rather than unease.

"I'm fine, now," she reassured. "I just need some coffee, then I'll perk back up."

"That, I can arrange."

The barista in the nearby coffee shop was beginning to know them by name, which made Stella feel even more attached to this place. She'd thought that the big city would be so impersonal—that was what she remembered hating about Atlanta, how lonely it could be. She'd felt like all she had was her little family. Sunrise Beach had been so different. Everyone knew one another, for better or worse. It meant there could be a lot of gossip, but it also made the place feel like home. What was that line from *Cheers*?

Where everybody knows your name...

Maybe she'd only felt so lonely in Atlanta because she hadn't known anyone she really liked. Seattle could be a different story for her, especially if she had Angela by her side. She still didn't know how Kelsey was going to take it, but based on how things were going so far, she was beginning to think it might be worth bringing up to her. Stella could do this, this lifestyle, and perhaps she wanted to. This could be, like Angela had promised, a gateway to riches, success, and the life she'd never even dared to dream of.

"How would you feel about watching a deal go down today?"

Stella blinked. "What kind of deal?" she asked. To her knowledge, Angela wasn't selling any artwork right now, so she was intrigued to be able to see something private that wasn't known to the general public.

"Something secret," she said. "There are things about this business that go on behind the scenes, things you need to learn to do and people you need to learn to talk to. It won't always be easy, but I want to show you because I had to figure it all out on my own, and it was a nightmare. I don't want that for you."

Stella had no idea what Angela was talking about, but followed her anyway to the cab that took them not to a café or diner like she'd expected, but to a hotel. All her questions were ignored with the promise of being answered soon enough as Stella followed Angela to the elevator, then to the tenth floor and down a series of long hallways until they arrived at the door of a room, where Angela knocked three times.

A man opened the door and Stella immediately recognized him as one of the museum directors in charge of the open museum slot that Angela was seeking.

"Nick," she greeted warmly. "It's so nice to see you. How have you been?"

"Oh, you know. Same old, same old." He eyed Stella up and down with suspicion. "You've brought a guest."

She nodded. "Stella is cool. I've taken her under my wing a bit, and I'm teaching her the ropes. Thought this might be an important thing for her to see."

"If you really believe she's trustworthy. I don't want her saying anything to anyone."

Angela turned to Stella, who was feeling more terrified by the minute, with a warm, reassuring smile. "What we're about to do here isn't strictly allowed, but it's not illegal or anything like that. The worst that would happen is that we would get blacklisted from doing exhibits or selling to certain people, and we really don't want that."

"What *are* we doing here, Angela? You still haven't explained."

Nick turned and went back into the room, leaving the door open for them to follow. Angela's voice was low when she spoke. "Nick is on the committee to vote for who gets that empty museum slot. Right now, they're leaning toward Vidhan, but it's close. Some of them are saying that he might be a bad choice because of the older crowd who don't use the internet, which just so happen to be a good majority of the people who come to tour these art museums."

"That sounds like it could bring in a lot of people who don't normally frequent the museum."

"Or," she pointed out, "It could cause a lot of regulars who won't get the appeal of the exhibit because they don't

Making Big Decisions

know he's internet famous and won't like the paintings. I'm hoping to convince Nick to make the latter argument for me at the meeting, and when they vote, if he can sway just one more person, it becomes a tie and the person above him decides on the spotlight exhibit."

Stella's jaw dropped. Was she bribing him? "And the person above Nick... Do you know him, too?"

Angela flashed a wicked smile. "I do." Before Stella could protest, she was ushered into the hotel suite and onto a sofa.

The room was enormous. Stella had stayed in nice hotel rooms before. Family members on both sides had pitched in to help her and Jeff afford a nice honeymoon suite after their wedding, and since then, on every family vacation, they'd purchased a nice family suite with Jeff's stolen money. Even still, this room was impressive. The ceilings were high and adorned with a chandelier, and there was a lot of furniture in the room, more than Stella had in her living room. The bed looked like it might be bigger than Stella's whole bedroom, though she knew that was a huge exaggeration.

"Wow," she couldn't help but breathe, and Nick smiled.

"Crazy room, right?"

"You can afford this on a museum curator's salary?"

Nick and Angela both laughed like it was a dumb question, and Stella felt her ears grow hot with embarrassment.

"Oh, honey," Angela said. "No. Nick has a side gig."

"What is it?"

Angela sat beside her on the sofa and Stella had the

distinct feeling that she was about to find out, and she wasn't going to like the answer.

"Paintings by painters who have been featured in the SAM spotlight exhibit always sell for more money, especially during and directly after their exhibit. When I know who is going to get the museum spot, I like to buy a few paintings before the price skyrockets, then sell them to auctions."

Stella frowned. "Isn't that like insider trading?"

Once more, Nick laughed, but this time, Stella could tell he was losing patience, as the sound wasn't kind or amused. "We're dealing in paintings, here, darling, not government secrets. It's not like I'm about to collapse the stock market. I'm making a little extra money on the side from artists who, usually, could stand to have some extra cash."

It felt dirty. She didn't want to be here, didn't want to be a person who dealt like this. Was this how Angela got her first spot? Had she been prepared to bribe Stella in this way if she had said no to her initial proposal?

"Oh, don't look so horrified," Angela teased. "Everyone does it. Sometimes, you have to break a few rules to get ahead, and we both deserve to get ahead."

For the entire deal, Stella sat still and silent. Angela gave Nick a ridiculous discount on a handful of paintings, however, they were still expensive enough that in order to turn a real profit, he would have to ensure that she held that spotlight exhibit. He promised her that he would fight for her as hard as he could, which Stella took to mean that he would at the very least vote so obstinately against Vidhan that they would have to appeal the decision to Angela's other friend, who would then side with her. She might have had the same deal going with that man, too. Stella could only imagine. All she knew was that she didn't like it. It made her ill at ease.

The worst of it was the feeling that this was just like what Jeff was doing behind her back all these years. Angela had sworn that she would help her rise to the top, but was this the cost? Would she have to allow her friend to step on the toes of other artists, many of whom were even more deserving of the fame than she was? She thought of Vidhan and his daughter, the chubby-cheeked girl of no more than five years old depicted in the article. The look on her face of excitement and wonderment brought her back to Kelsey's childhood, when she would watch Stella paint with awe in her eyes. Stella would ask her what she wanted painted and then create it, no matter what it was. She painted their house too many times to count, as well as Gwen's home (which Kelsey affectionately referred to as "Gammaw's"), the park near their house that Stella took Kelsey to play, and even fantasy worlds that existed only in Kelsey's head.

Angela was right. Less skill had gone into those paintings. She'd never been able to sell them, had never even tried. Still, she kept them in the back of her closet and looked at them when she was feeling particularly nostalgic. In that way, she might have regarded them as the most beautiful works of art she had created in her whole career. Vidhan deserved every ounce of fame he got for sharing his story, and Stella was not willing to participate in taking that away from him, even if she did believe that Angela was a better artist.

Jeff had been willing to go behind her back and make decisions for her that she didn't agree with, and she wasn't willing to enter into that same sort of agreement with Angela. Not to mention, if she was attempting to teach Stella to do this, would she expect her to repay the favor someday? No, she thought, it was better to shut it down now before things got out of hand.

Stella texted Kelsey to call her with some fake emergency while Angela was driving her back to their hotel, ensuring that she would be within earshot when the call came through. When she did, Kelsey made up something about not feeling well and thinking that she might have to go to the hospital to have her appendix out. Stella knew it wasn't true, since Kelsey was really just retelling the story of how that had happened when she was fourteen, but it still evoked an emotion in Stella that was strong enough to apparently make the performance believable.

"Is she okay?" Angela asked after Stella hung up, and Stella shook her head.

"The doctors think she might need her appendix out. I hate to do this, but—"

"No, of course, you need to fly home. I'll get you a ticket on the next plane to South Carolina. There will be a car waiting, too, to take you directly home. Or to the hospital, if that's what you prefer."

"No, that's okay. She wants me to bring her an overnight bag, anyway. I really appreciate this, Angela. I'll pay you back."

"Nonsense. The trip was all-expenses paid. Or did you think I was planning on trapping you here?"

Stella forced a laugh, now unsure if she would even put

that past Angela. "I just feel bad. At least let me pay for the price of moving the ticket up."

Angela waved off the suggestion, making Stella regret having used such a sympathetic excuse. She should have just bit the bullet and told Angela she wanted to go home, but that had felt rude. It wasn't Angela's fault, not exactly, and she had gone through all this trouble to fly her out here. All she knew for sure was that she was no longer interested in moving here, at least not to start a business with Angela. She'd had enough involvement in shady business practices for one lifetime.

Chapter Ten

On the plane ride home, Stella watched the city of Seattle below her until the rain clouds obscured her view. It was a miracle that the weather had even cleared up for long enough to allow her to take the next plane, since it had looked especially gloomy all morning. Angela had somehow managed to find her a spot on a plane leaving that afternoon, and though she'd barely made it to the terminal in time to board, she could now breathe easy knowing that she was heading home.

Now with Angela no longer beside her to distract her from her thoughts on the plane, her mind wandered. She'd been downgraded from first class, but Stella certainly didn't mind. She didn't need to fly first class, anyway, and if it meant that she could get home sooner, she would have volunteered to tuck herself away with the luggage. She had no idea what she was going to tell Kelsey, whether she would go into the whole story about the underhanded deal, how she'd wanted no part in something that felt so dubiously legal and certainly amoral. Kelsey had been rooting for her. She'd encouraged her to go out on this trip, something that was so far out of her comfort zone, and now it was ruined.

She ordered a glass of wine on the plane because her mind was reeling. Not only had someone that she trusted done something awful yet again, but she hadn't realized just how much she'd allowed herself to dream of a life here. It hadn't been intentional, and she hadn't even really realized that she was doing it, but Angela's plan had worked. She'd been able to picture herself in those coffee shops and museums, hanging out with those fun artists in bars and learning about their lives. She was going to miss it, but more than anything, it had been exhausting. She wasn't sure if she would be able to do something like that long term. The only thing she knew for sure was that she was going to be in charge of her own career from now on and didn't need anyone to help boost her up. She'd come this far on her own. She had started her own gallery, held her own exhibits, and even caught the attention of a famous artist without anyone's help. Her students were waiting for her, as well.

When Stella walked in the door, exhausted from her trip and the long flight, she didn't even bother putting her luggage away. Angela had told her to keep the clothes she'd bought for her, which had made her feel even worse about the lie. She tried to force herself to rally and stay out the remainder of the weekend, but she just couldn't bring herself to do it. She couldn't get excited about Seattle with this dark cloud hanging over her head.

Making Big Decisions

In the end, Stella ended up deciding not to tell Kelsey that she'd come home early at all. It was only two more days, after all, and she'd been so looking forward to staying with Mariah. Angela's all-expenses-paid vacation had included a hefty payment to Mariah's family for providing her with food and lodging, so she didn't feel too guilty about that. She used the time alone to paint. She'd taken a lot of pictures in Seattle, and though she hadn't gotten to paint the National Parks while she was there like she'd hoped, that didn't mean she couldn't do her best to do so working from the photographs she'd taken.

They'd not gone far into the park, but Angela had taken her on a short, quick hike early in the morning, and she'd taken a lot of pictures. Stella decided that it would be risky to head into town and paint in her gallery studio, since she didn't want it getting back to Mariah's parents that she had returned early and not told them and come to pick up her daughter. Instead, she decided to head back up to her tiny studio in the cottage, where she hung up her favorite photo of the park. It was right after sunrise, and she'd fallen in love with the way the sun had filtered through the needles of the fir trees. This would be the first time she would ever paint a tree like that. She was used to mostly palm trees, and the texture provided a new challenge for her. Finding the right color was new, too, deeper and darker green than she typically used for painting nature. It felt exciting to try her hand at a landscape that had been so foreign to her.

Stella lost herself in her painting for hours, not noticing how the rain was pelting the window. She supposed that she'd grown used to it in Washington and had learned to tune it out. There, it had been a sort of constant background noise. The clouds waxed and waned, the storm passing and raging in time with her rolling thoughts. She couldn't stop thinking about Angela, how she'd trusted her and watched it blow up in her face. Was there something about Stella that attracted these people, people who wanted to take the easy way out and felt the need to take her with them?

Of course, as she usually did when she was feeling particularly upset, she thought about Jeff. Though the trees looked nothing like those in Atlanta, she still found herself thinking of their old house, the one she'd had to pack up and leave in a hurry, never to return. They had bought the house together with the intention of raising their kids there, years ago. Through they'd always thought about having more than one, the house had always felt full with Kelsey running around by herself. She'd never been a lonely child, and her constant chatter and tendency to follow her parents around the house singing and dancing had made it so they never felt like anything was missing.

As she painted, she began to see her life with Jeff in a new light. He had been different from Angela. She was self-serving, and while her crime had certainly been more forgivable, her motive had not. Jeff had always felt as though he was doing what he did for his family, in his own twisted way, and Stella couldn't fault him for that.

"Wouldn't you do everything in your power to ensure that Kelsey has a good future ahead of her?" he'd asked her shortly after his arrest, when she was still speaking to him on the phone. After that call, she'd stopped picking up.

"She had a good future, a good life," she replied furiously. *"You ruined that for her."*

Now, looking at how happy Kelsey was with Marco and all her new friends, seeing how she was loving science and succeeding in school and about to start her internship, Stella wasn't so sure she still felt that way. He hadn't ruined anything. He didn't have the power, because she'd always been there to pick up the pieces.

The most valuable thing that Stella had learned in Seattle had been the marketing tips taught to her by Angela's team. She'd been allowed to sit in on a few meetings about selling Angela as a person rather than just her art, and it had been a concept that was foreign to Stella. She'd always tried to let her work speak for itself. Her website was proof enough of that, just a gallery of images and her contact information. However, the marketing agents had warned against that.

"People can get a painting from anywhere. Unless they're an art critic or a collector, they're not going to be able to see subtle differences in technique. The average person couldn't tell a Monet from a Manet. If they're going to pay a premium price for something, they want to feel good about their purchase, and that starts with you."

She decided to start with her website. When she'd set it up, she'd opted against having an "about me" section, but now she felt that it was time to add one. Pouring herself a tall glass of wine, Stella sat down to her laptop with a pad of scratch paper and a pen and began drafting the perfect bio. Was it tacky to start with how many years she'd been painting, or did people want to know that? Would it make her sound experienced, or pretentious? Should she talk about her divorce, since it was the biggest factor in what had made her start to take painting more seriously, or was that too much personal information to disclose? The line between too casual and overly formal was surprisingly thin, and she found herself fluctuating between both. Her head was spinning, and the whole time, she felt self-conscious, knowing that everyone she knew would read this and know what she thought was most important to present about herself.

The paragraph she ended up with wasn't the perfect summary she'd hoped for. However, it was a start, so when she finally got approval from Felicia, she published it to the site. It was a level of vulnerability that she hadn't been able to display in a long time for fear of her past catching up with her, and it was equal parts liberating and terrifying.

"It's a step in the right direction," Felicia reassured her as she poured her a glass of wine. She'd refused to drink any while she was working on the paragraph, but now, her evening was free. Felicia held her glass out to toast: "To letting yourself be known, even just a little." Stella toasted back and took a long sip of wine.

"It feels good. I've been hiding for a long time, it feels like. Since Jeff, I've struggled to let anyone in. I'm working on that."

"Speaking of letting people know you," Felicia said. "I heard from Graham yesterday. He's finally found a new client. He's been utterly rudderless since the contract with the Frenchman didn't get renewed."

Stella tried to hide her interest, knowing that Felicia

would make it out to be less innocent than it really was. She missed Graham, of course, but she knew that what they had had always been temporary. Any feelings that she'd developed for him were under control. Now, she was trying to view him more as Felicia's older brother rather than her own ex-fling, but the transition wasn't easy. She still thought about him often. Though the goal had been simply to open the door to dating other men again after Jeff had hurt her so deeply, she found that she didn't really want to date anyone else. When she thought about going on dates, she wanted Graham to be there.

Perhaps she was overthinking it. It was natural to have stronger feelings for the first man who had taken interest in her since her divorce, she thought, and Stella hadn't ever dated much. Jeff had been her first and only serious boyfriend, and she'd married him right out of high school. They had both been so young. Now she was older, but she reminded herself that she still had tons of options. There were plenty of fish in the sea, after all, and she'd barely even cast out a line.

"That's wonderful to hear. Where's this client based?"

"Not in the States, if that's what you're wondering," Felicia replied sadly. "I'm afraid it'll be a while before he has reason to visit here again for work."

Stella hadn't been wondering that specifically, but she did find herself disappointed to hear the news. A part of her had been hoping that he would come back to visit, she realized. She leaned against the back of Felicia's black leather couch and sighed. "Do you ever think about going back to England to visit your family? How long has it been since you traveled there?"

Felicia shook her head vehemently. "Oh, heavens, no. I'm terrified of flying. I do it as little as I can. My whole family knows that if they want to see me, they must come to me. I haven't been back in years."

Stella frowned. "That's awful. Don't you miss it?"

"Of course I do," she replied, then sighed. "I'm sure someday I'll be able to get over the fear, but for now, it's simply insurmountable."

Stella couldn't believe that she was hearing this from Felicia, the fiercest person she'd ever met. Every time Stella had expressed a fear to her, she'd encouraged her to face it head on, to not let nerves stand in her way of achieving her dreams. Perhaps this was why: she had her own anxieties that prevented her from doing the things she wanted to do.

"If you ever want a flying buddy," Stella offered, "I would be more than happy to go with you." Felicia smirked, successfully hiding the expression that had begun to grow slightly sad behind a wicked, pleased mask.

"Oh? I'll have to take you up on that someday." She glanced down at her watch and gasped, a put-upon gesticulation that Stella knew meant that she wanted some time to herself. "Is it that late already? I hate to kick you out, but I'm helping the girls open tomorrow. Lilly is still out on maternity leave, you know, so they've needed an extra pair of hands."

Stella nodded and stood, thankful that she hadn't had time to sip much of her wine. "I completely understand. I've got to get home to Kelsey, anyway. It was nice to see you, Felicia. And thanks for the help on the website. You're a real lifesaver."

She grinned. "Anytime! I should be free for lunch all

Making Big Decisions

this week, so if you want to stop by, feel free." Well, at least now she knew that Felicia wasn't upset with her for inadvertently bringing up a subject that was apparently somewhat sensitive.

"I'll text you."

Chapter Eleven

A week later, Stella was sweeping the gallery when her phone buzzed. Her heart sank when she recognized the phone number on the screen as that of Kelsey's college. With her mind already racing through possibilities of what might have happened to her daughter that was so serious she hadn't been able to call her herself, Stella answered the phone with trembling hands.

"Hello?"

"Is this Stella Britton?" a woman's voice, too cheerful to be announcing horrible news about her daughter being injured or ill, asked. Stella allowed herself to relax slightly.

"Yes, speaking. Is everything all right with my daughter?"

The woman hesitated. "Your daughter?"

"This is Sunrise Beach Community College, isn't it?"

"Oh!" the woman realized. "Oh, yes, I'm so sorry. Your daughter is fine, Ms. Britton. I did know she attends college here, but it slipped my mind. I'm sorry about that."

"That's all right," she breathed, weak with relief. "Is there something I can do for you, Ms...?"

"Meredith White!" she chirped. "You can call me Merry. I'm the school's chairperson for the art's department. How are you doing today?"

"Um, I'm all right, Merry. Can I ask what this is in reference to?"

"Well, forgive me if I'm overstepping, here, but I've heard great things about you. We have a couple of students, both your daughter's age and some nontraditional students who are retired, who have just gushed about how wonderful your classes are. I've seen some incredible work out of the students who say they started painting in your classes. I found your number through your website and was wondering if I could ask you a few questions."

Stella laughed, feeling the last bit of apprehension drain from her. "Of course. I'd be happy to answer anything you'd like."

"Excellent! Well, I suppose there's no point in beating around the bush, so my first question is, have you ever thought about teaching in a classroom setting rather than your current setup in your own gallery?"

Stella blinked a few times in surprise. "Um, I'm not sure I understand where you're going with that."

"Well, you see, we had a contract with a man who used to teach some evening classes here, but he retired this year. We've been looking for someone to fill his place. Since I heard about your classes, I've been really interested in learning more. Would you be interested in speaking about a role like that, if it were potentially available?"

Calling on everything she learned from Angela, Stella

restrained her excitement even though she wanted to squeal. "Sure, I have a bit of a break. That sounds interesting."

A steady job, one in her field, might just be falling into her lap, and all she had to do was answer a few questions? It sounded too good to be true.

"Well, our night classes are a bit different from what your daughter might be used to. Most of the students in those classes aren't on a degree path, and those who are usually aren't taking many art classes, though some of them might be trying to fill electives. Mostly, the evening classes are for nontraditional students. That might include retired folks, people who want to learn a new skill but aren't enrolled in a degree program, and students who are working toward a degree but have to work during the day. They're a unique and amazing group of people, and we value them every bit as much as our traditional students."

Stella nodded. She remembered taking classes at a community college herself when Kelsey had just been born. After the birth of her first child, she became engrossed in the baby bubble. Nothing could pop it. She'd stopped showering, her friends hadn't seen her in weeks, and she barely slept. Jeff had become worried about her, but she'd assured him that she simply loved their baby more than she'd ever loved anything or anyone and wanted to be with her all the time.

"I just think it might be healthy for you to find something else you love, too," he'd suggested. "You know, get yourself out of the house a bit. Have an adult conversation. All this baby talk is going to get really lonely, I think, especially since I've been working so much lately."

He'd been right, of course. After a few weeks, Stella had started to grow restless during the day. She took Kelsey in her stroller out for coffee, which she still couldn't drink because she was breastfeeding, or to the park, where she would sit on the bench and watch the women who were enrolled in things like Pilates classes or walking clubs. She'd tried a few of those, but none had stuck. She was still too sore from her C-section to jog with the women around the neighborhood, and she quickly found out that she wasn't interested in yoga.

"Maybe I should go back to working part time," she'd suggested to Jeff's mother, Gwen, but she'd frowned.

"You said you didn't want to do that," she'd reminded her. "I mean, if you want to work, I support you, but you told me that you wanted to be able to choose your schedule and not have to be away from the baby for twenty hours a week. It's a big commitment."

She'd sighed. "I know, but I have to do *something*. I started talking to the neighbor's dog today, Gwen. I'm going to lose it if I don't start making some adult friends." She put down the newspaper she'd been reading at the kitchen table and slid a page toward Stella.

"What about something like this?" she'd asked. It was an advertisement for an art program at the community college, and at first she'd laughed, shaking her head.

"I'm not looking to go back to school. That's an even bigger commitment than a job."

"I don't think that's what this is. I think you can just choose to take a class or two, if you want. You've always liked painting, haven't you? Why don't you call up there tomorrow and see if you could take a painting class? Doesn't that sound like fun?"

Checking the classes out had been the best decision she'd ever made. From that class, she'd learned that she didn't just like painting, she loved it, and she was good at it. That teacher had been the one to encourage her to keep going even when she felt as though she hated everything she made. Without that conversation, she never would have learned just how much she could achieve, and she owed a lot of that to the night-school teacher who had believed in her. The idea of being able to do that for someone else brought a smile to her face.

The past rushed through her mind as she remembered that she'd been one of those non-traditional students that Merry was referring to. She smiled into the phone, wanting to share a fraction of her experience with the woman who might eventually offer her a job.

"I'm familiar with the type of class you're referring to," she said. "They changed my life, after my daughter was born. I think affordable art classes are so important to the community."

Merry was ecstatic to hear that. "I feel exactly the same way!" she exclaimed. "I'm so happy to hear you think that. Well, if you wanted to, I've got an open slot two nights a week that I'm really in a tight spot trying to fill, and I really think you might be perfect for it. I know you're probably really busy. I know you just had a recent exhibit with *THE* Angela Goff. But we can discuss salary and everything—"

"I would love to talk about filling the slot," Stella interjected, trying to remind herself of what Angela had told her. Play it cool and don't sound overeager, but at the same time, never let an opportunity slip through your fingers, and if there's something you want, grab it with both hands. Well, this was Stella grabbing. "When is a good time for me to come for an interview?"

By the end of the call, Stella had an appointment to interview the following afternoon, since it was her only morning off from classes, and felt ready. Normally, these sorts of things made her too nervous to be able to sleep, but tonight, she felt so prepared that she was asleep before her head even hit the pillow. She needed her rest if she was going to nail the interview the next morning.

The interview turned out to be a formality, really. As soon as Stella showed up at the arts building of the College, she was greeted by Merry, who looked different from what Stella had expected over the phone. She'd expected an older woman to be the head of the department, but Merry was young, with short, asymmetrical hair that was dyed jet black with blue highlights. She looked more like a student than a member of staff, but Stella wasn't going to say anything about that.

It was quick. After Merry took her back to her office and offered her a cup of coffee, which Stella would normally refuse but took because she knew that Angela would, she asked her a few questions about her background. Stella answered them as best she could without giving too much away. She told Merry she was originally from a tiny town in Alabama, that her parents had moved her to Atlanta for her father's job and that she'd only come to Sunrise Beach permanently after her divorce. Luckily, Merry wasn't the nosy type and didn't pry too much into the divorce. In fact, she seemed a bit uncomfortable and was eager to change the subject. Stella told her about her education, specifically her community college classes and how she was self-taught for a lot of her technique. From there, she went into her teaching background, and by the end of it, Merry was looking at her with stars in her eyes. She looked almost in love. *They must have really been panicking about how they were going to replace this professor*, Stella figured.

"Well, from your experience alone, it sounds like you would be a great fit. Not to mention the fact that your name is pretty well known around here. I think there are a lot of people who might sign up for classes just because they hear you're teaching them. It might even be an incentive to be able to expand the department's budget. Of course, that's all hypothetical. I'm just... wishful thinking."

Stella smiled. "Of course. I'm interested in the position. I love teaching, but it's been a lot of work to have to advertise my own classes and find a place for everyone. I've been having to turn a lot of students away because my studio can only fit a handful of people at a time."

"Then it sounds like we'd be good for one another!" Merry said. "When can you start?"

Chapter Twelve

Stella found herself waiting up later and later for Kelsey to return home. Ever since things had begun to get more serious between her and Marco, Stella had started imposing rules on sleepovers. No sleeping over with friends on school nights, and Kelsey had to send her proof that she was really with her friends rather than sneaking out with her boyfriend. It wasn't that she didn't trust Kelsey, but she'd been a teenage girl once, and she remembered how it was. She'd thought she knew everything, and it wasn't until she looked back on her choices and felt regret for having rushed into a serious relationship that she really saw just how stupid she'd been. Now, Stella would have given anything to have spared herself and Kelsey that heartbreak, but all she could really do was try to prevent Kelsey from making the same mistakes.

She wasn't sure if it were nature or nurture, but Kelsey was a lot like her mother in a lot of ways. For starters, she was ambitious. Once she set her mind to something, there was no changing her mind, not for anything. Just like her mother, she cared deeply for the people she loved. Either of them would give the shirts off their backs to help someone that they cared about. Finally, and perhaps most dangerously, Kelsey had her mother's inherent trust of people. Stella considered herself an optimist, possibly to a fault. She assumed people's good intentions and was always equal parts hurt and shocked when they turned around and hurt her. Jeff's betrayal had been the worst, but Stella couldn't count how many times in her lifetime she'd found out that she had been being used by a friend or relative, especially after they'd found out she'd gotten rich. She was a bleeding heart, and so was Kelsey.

"Hey, Mom," Kelsey greeted on Friday morning, more chipper than Stella was used to seeing her. "I think I'm going to go out after school tonight." Ever since she'd agreed to let Marco give her a ride to school in the mornings, she'd been waking up more easily. What had once been a fight to get Kelsey out of bed every day had mellowed out. In fact, most days, Kelsey was already sitting at the breakfast table eating her cereal by the time Stella returned from her jog. The only problem was that, now, Kelsey spent a lot more time in their shared bathroom doing her hair and makeup, which meant that Stella had to wait to use the shower when she returned hot and sweaty from her run.

"Where to?" Stella asked, trying to sound conversational. "Who's all going to be there?"

Kelsey rolled her eyes. "Enough with the third degree. I'm just going out with Marco. It's our three-month anniversary, and he wants to go to a nice restaurant downtown."

Stella almost laughed. "You two are celebrating monthly anniversaries?"

"Everyone does it," she shrugged. "Three months is a long time. It's longer than I've ever dated anyone before, anyway."

Stella wanted to remind her that she'd never really dated *anyone* before. Kelsey had never been in a serious relationship. The most experience that she'd had was a few dates she'd gotten for dances in high school. They had called themselves her boyfriend for a few weeks before she politely told them she wasn't interested in taking things further. All her life, she'd been so focused on her studies that she'd never felt like she had time for dating. Before, Stella had always encouraged her to ease up on herself, cajoling her to have some fun and not be so terribly obsessed with her grades. She did well on tests whether she studied for an hour or a week, so there was no reason, Stella had persuaded, for her to drive herself crazy with stress.

However, she knew that saying any of that to Kelsey would upset her, or worse, make her angry. They'd been getting along so well lately, ever since Stella eased up on some of her house rules and gave Kelsey a bit more freedom. She was a good kid, Stella knew, and smart. She could handle herself. Stella just hated to see her setting herself up to be hurt. She still wasn't fully sold on Marco, either. While he seemed like a nice enough guy, there were flashes where Stella didn't think the two were perfectly suited for one another. What Kelsey called confidence, Stella worried might be cockiness. The decisive nature Kelsey loved could cross the line into stubbornness, which her sweet daughter was susceptible to giving in to.

"Well, I won't stop you. How nice of a restaurant are we talking, here?"

Kelsey laughed. "Why, are you trying to tag along?"

"I might, if Marco's footing the bill!"

Kelsey rolled her eyes again, but there was no malice to it. That had been absent, lately, and their relationship had felt so much friendlier. However, Stella was still her mother, and she didn't want to neglect her duty to protect her daughter in favor of preserving the peace.

"I'll text you when we leave. We might hang out a bit afterward, depending on what movies are playing."

"Sure. Just let me know, and don't stay out too late. Curfew is still eleven, even on an 'anniversary.'"

Stella turned to head into her studio upstairs to get some work done, but Kelsey sighed. "Hey, Mom, wait up a second."

"What is it, honey?"

Kelsey paused, seemingly trying to choose her words carefully. "I wanted some advice, actually."

"Of course, sweetie. What about?"

"How old were you when you moved in with Dad?"

Stella's heart sank thinking that Kelsey was already wondering about things like this with Marco. They'd only been dating for three months, for Pete's sake. How could she already be thinking about something like that with him?

"Well, you know that my situation with your dad was... unique. I had nowhere to go when my parents passed, and your Grandma took me in. We technically started living together when I was nineteen, but in reality, we didn't move out until I was twenty-one. Even that, I think, was too early, but it was difficult living with your grandmother. We wanted to give her space."

Kelsey didn't appear to love that answer, but nodded to signify that she was listening, at least. "Do you ever want space?"

Her eyebrows furrowed in surprise. "No, honey, of course not. I'd be so lonely living on my own here. Why do you ask?" she asked, as if the answer weren't obvious.

"I've just been thinking about some things," she dodged. "Mariah is thinking of getting her own apartment. I've gone with her to look at a few, and some of the places around here are really cool. With the money I'd be making from the internship, I could probably comfortably afford half of a rent payment for a one-bedroom. They're actually paying the hourly rate of a lab tech. It's not much, but it's something."

The "half a rent payment" didn't escape Stella's notice, but she didn't dare ask who she was thinking of moving into a one bedroom apartment with. Perhaps she was thinking of moving in with one of her friends. She knew that was too optimistic, but she had to give Kelsey the benefit of the doubt.

"Well, just remember to be sure before you decide anything. Leases are a year long, and they can be really tough to get out of if something happens." Truth be told, she didn't love the idea of her daughter living with a man she wasn't married to, but she wasn't sure if that was better or worse than the thought of Kelsey getting married. She couldn't impose that rule because it could have the opposite of its intended effect and push her into a more serious relationship rather than making her slow her roll with Marco.

She told herself that this was normal for girls Kelsey's age. They were only just starting dating. She would spend a few more weeks with this guy and get out of the honeymoon phase. Little habits would begin to irritate her—Kelsey had a lot of pet peeves, anyway. There was no way she would survive living with a boy that, in reality, she barely knew.

Kelsey headed back to her room without another word, leaving Stella sitting at the kitchen table with a glass of orange juice and what felt like a brick in her stomach. She always felt that way when she worried. Her mother used to have it, too, that nervous stomach that made it feel impossible to eat anything. Jeff had always been the opposite, a stress eater. He always used to say how lucky she was, since he always seemed to gain weight right before an important client interview or when Kelsey would travel with her friends for a spring break trip. She wondered distantly what he looked like now. Had being on a strict prison diet prevented him from snacking during the divorce, or would he have that familiar roundness to his cheeks that she had come to associate with troubled times?

She didn't want to think about Jeff right now, so she jammed the thought down and finished her juice before heading to her studio, this time with a painting in mind.

Chapter Thirteen

On the following Monday, Stella's phone buzzed with a phone call that made her heart race just as it had the first time, but now, it was for different reasons. Angela Goff was once again contacting her.

She wasn't sure why she was surprised. Though her excuse to leave Seattle had been flimsy at best, she'd never lied to Angela before, and she had given no indication that she hadn't believed her when she'd said that Kelsey was ill. Part of her had thought that because she hadn't texted to check in, she had seen through the ruse. Stella was currently working through a theory that involved Angela having seen Kelsey posing with her friends on Instagram while she should have, according to Stella's story, been recovering from surgery in the hospital. Did she really have to answer?

"Angela, hi," she greeted, biting back the tone of discontent. "I'm sorry I haven't called."

"No, that's my fault," Angela replied. "I never really know what to do or say when people deal with... this sort of thing, you know? It's so awkward, and I'm terrible at being comforting. I'm not the nurturing type, I guess, but I've been thinking about you. How's your daughter?"

Stella breathed a sigh of both relief and irritation, having been halfway hoping she'd rid herself of this problem with one obvious lie that Angela had seen through. She wasn't terribly sure that she wanted to continue to be friends with someone who worked the way Angela did, and she certainly didn't want to intertwine her business with these shady practices.

"She's doing much better," she said. "Thank you."

"Oh, wow, am I so glad to hear that. I bet you've been having a stressful week, huh?"

Stella's agreement wasn't even a lie. Things had been difficult this week, though not for the reasons she'd said.

"Well, I want to do something nice for you. How about we go out for lunch tomorrow? I'm back in the city and would love to see you."

Stella hesitated. "I'm not sure, Angela. I'm really not in the mood to be thinking about—"

"We won't talk about work stuff, I promise. Gossip and gab only. I think we've been missing out on that for a while. What do you say? Are you free?"

While Stella wasn't sure how much she believed Angela could get through a lunch without bringing up work, she agreed simply because she didn't have a good excuse not to go. The sick kid excuse had already been used in a major way, and if she made up a different lie, Angela would certainly think she was avoiding her. She was, of course, but she didn't like the idea of Angela thinking that. That was something Stella knew about herself. She could never be rude to someone, even if it might be in her best interests.

"Sure. I'll meet you at the Townsend Café at noon, all right?" At least then Felicia would be there to bail her out if she really needed to get out of there.

To Stella's shock, Angela was true to her word about not bringing up work at their lunch. Felicia had even been invited to sit at the table by Angela when it became clear that she was Stella's friend, so that helped to steer the conversation away from art in general. Rather, they recounted some stories from the trip to Seattle. Felicia had never been and feigned interest even though Stella doubted she really wanted to know about the best restaurants and worst cafés in a city she'd never visited.

"We went to this bar," Angela said, laughing into her tea. Stella immediately began to giggle, feeling her cheeks heat up in embarrassment.

"Don't tell this one!"

"Please, whatever it is, I must know," Felicia encouraged.

"It was my fault, really. I knew this place did line dancing, but I misread the website. I thought it said it was only on Thursday nights, but it turned out that it was every night except Thursdays. So, we showed up on a Friday, empty stomachs and wearing heels, to this bar where everyone is standing in the middle of the floor wearing cowboy hats."

"No!" Felicia gasped. "I assume you both left."

"Would I be telling you this if we had?"

Stella flushed an even deeper red. "We'd already paid the door price, which included two drinks, so it's not like we were just going to leave without getting our money's worth. I told Angela that we could drink there, but there would be absolutely no dancing, and that I wasn't wearing a hat."

Just to undermine her, Angela dug through her pockets to pull out her phone, where she scrolled through her photo album until she arrived at one of Stella in a bright pink cowboy hat on top of a mechanical bull. She couldn't believe that it was really a picture of herself, looking at it. Having lived as a high-society suburban housewife for the past several decades, something like this wasn't anything she'd ever expected herself to do. She had always considered it to be far too embarrassing to try, like having a little tipsy fun was below her.

"Well, of course the first thing I did was buy both of us a hat," Angela said. "The second thing was to guilt Stella into putting it on."

"How did you get her on that bull?"

She laughed. "I think the third margarita finished the job I started. I just kept telling her how fun it would be until finally, she stood up and just... got up there!"

"I figured it was better than line dancing," she said. "At least I ran the risk of breaking my neck and getting out of that bar."

"Does this look like the face of someone who didn't have an amazing time setting the bar's record for longest bull ride in high heels?" Angela zoomed in on her face in the photo for good measure. She was grinning, laughing. She really had enjoyed herself, even if it wasn't something she could ever see herself doing again. It was the kind of night that she had only agreed to because it was Angela Goff, and she didn't regret a moment of it.

The conversation continued, Angela telling more stories about the trip and asking Felicia questions about her own travels, probably mentally making notes for where she wanted to host future art exhibits. Stella zoned out a bit, since she was no longer considering having another exhibit with Angela. It pained her to think that way, but she just couldn't put herself through that again. Jeff's involvement in shady business had ruined her life and reputation. Now, she was finally doing what she wanted to do in life. If someone or something were to take this away from her, it would be possibly more devastating than simply losing her big house in the nicest suburb of Atlanta. She'd worked so hard for this, which meant that she was going to protect it with everything she had.

Angela didn't bring up the exhibit or the plans they had been discussing before she'd hightailed it home. True to her word, she kept the conversation light and fun. Stella began to wonder if she didn't have to sacrifice her friendship with Angela, after all. She'd been sure that by turning her down and informing her she didn't want to go into business with her, she would be ensuring that Angela would never talk to her again. The two only became acquainted in the first place because Angela had liked Stella's art and wanted to work with her, and the friendship had only continued from there because Stella had thought that sounded like a dream come true. Now that she wasn't so sure, she anticipated that Angela might move on to the next prospective partner and never speak to her again. Their easy bonding now made her think that maybe there was something real in their friendship, something beyond a potential business deal.

In the following days, Stella, despite her growing confidence that she could maintain a relationship with Angela even if they weren't business partners, avoided her. Things felt fragile, and she didn't want to risk the topic of their nearly disastrous trip coming up again. She felt as though she was just buying time before she would have to explain what had really brought her back to Sunrise Beach in such a hurry. Which also meant that she would have to denounce Angela's business practices even though many of them had directly benefited her. Angela would doubtlessly defend herself, which would make Stella relive unpleasant memories of the day that Jeff had been arrested.

Hearing his defensive voice in her head was one of the side effects of what Jeff had done. She tried to push the words away, but the familiar soundtrack played anyway.

"I wasn't hurting anyone."

"Everyone makes some questionable choices to get ahead in this business."

"I just didn't see another way to the top."

The same tired excuses would be recycled again and again, and she was afraid that if she heard them from Angela's mouth, she wouldn't be able to look her in the eye again.

Chapter Fourteen

Rather than dwell on hypothetical arguments with Angela and old wounds with Jeff, Stella decided to throw herself headfirst into yet another project. Her most advanced gallery class was coming to an end, and she could tell they were envious of the treatment that her last advanced class had gotten, namely the exhibit she'd done with them. Their art and hers had all been sold together, which had made a pretty penny for both herself and all of her students featured in the gallery. Though they'd only been able to sell their art for a modest price, most of them had never sold a piece in their lives, and it had been a dream come true to have someone like their art enough to want to purchase it. She could tell based on how many questions her students were beginning to ask about the exhibit that they wanted to have one of their own.

"I know you've been dropping hints," she said at the end of her class. Her most boisterous student, a young, recently divorced dad named Tim, feigned ignorance. He always showed up to class wearing cargo shorts and a

Hawaiian shirt, a wardrobe he said embarrassed his daughter when he dropped her off at school. She was still in middle school, much younger than Kelsey, but Stella felt a special connection with Tim because of their shared experience in having to make the choice to split up the family of a teenage girl. His daughter, Laron, was handling it about as well as Kelsey had in the beginning, and he often came to Stella for advice on how to handle it.

"Hints?" he asked despite being the biggest perpetrator. "I have no idea what you're talking about. Hints at what?"

"Art exhibits take a lot of time and energy to plan. I love to do them, but every time I do, I feel like I need a full year to prepare myself mentally before even attempting another."

Tim smirked. "But...?"

She rolled her eyes. "But," she finished, "I've been inspired by all of you. I think the most tiring part of this for me is always painting a whole new set of works to be displayed beside yours. I was thinking today, though, why would I need to do that? I mean, my name is already on the building, so it's not like you'd be losing out on any notoriety if I didn't display some new set I've put together just for this event, right?"

A middle-aged woman named Carrie, who Stella was pretty sure was dating Tim on the down low, frowned, her pretty brown hair bobbing as she tilted her head to the side. "You're not serious. An exhibit? Really?"

"You've all earned it. You've worked so hard, I would hate to deprive you of the experience. Plus, I did it with my last semester students, so fair is fair, right?" The logic tracked, but she would sooner change her name and flee the country than throw a new exhibit every six weeks for the rest of her life. Maybe she could work out a different kind of show they could all put together in place of something so expensive and exhausting.

The news was met with giddy cheers. Though the thought of putting it together in a mad dash once again was stressful, Stella became more confident each time she did so. She was learning what corners she could cut, what little details made the exhibit feel more professional for a low price, and how to advertise. The advertisement and catering were always the hardest parts, and even those she was beginning to perfect into a science.

"We can help set it up!" Carrie insisted. "It'll be a learning experience, and I've always wanted to be an event planner, anyway. You don't have to do this all by yourself. We'd never ask for that, right, guys?"

With varying degrees of enthusiasm, the group agreed, leaving Stella with little to do for the exhibit other than offer pointers and help advertise. For that part, Angela was more than happy to oblige. Stella didn't actually ask her for help—she was afraid to owe Angela a favor. Angela couldn't be stopped. Once she had read about the exhibit on Stella's website, she'd called her immediately, not even offering a greeting when Stella picked up the phone.

"Why didn't you tell me you were throwing another exhibit?" she asked, or rather, demanded. Her tone wasn't exactly angry, but Stella could tell she wasn't pleased, and she tried to rack her brain for an excuse she could give that was better than, "I didn't want you involved."

"Well, my students have been really insistent on doing everything themselves." Not quite a lie, but not the whole truth. They had only insisted on taking some of the burden off Stella, but if Angela had offered to step in and provide pointers or even some help, they would have been chomping at the bit to reap the benefits. "I didn't want to send the message that I didn't think they could do it."

"Hmm," Angela hummed. Stella wasn't sure whether or not she'd convinced her with the lame excuse, but in typical Angela fashion, she steamrolled ahead, anyway. "I won't tell anyone, then. Just between you and me, though, I've invited a few people. You don't have to tell your students anything about it. Just act surprised when they show up."

"What?" Stella stammered. "Who? What kind of people?"

She could practically hear Angela break into a grin on the other end of the line. "Maybe it's better I don't tell you. That way, you won't have to fake it on the night of the gallery. You're a great artist, but not much of an actress."

Stella wondered distantly if that was a dig, if Angela somehow knew that she had lied to her to get out of Seattle, but she shook her head to clear that thought away. If Angela suspected that, she would confront her. She wasn't exactly the type to beat around the bush.

"Angela, I really don't know about this. My work isn't even going to be featured in this exhibit, you know. It's only the art of my students. I don't want professional critics there making them feel self-conscious."

"Oh, ye of little faith," Angela admonished. "I didn't invite critics. Of course I didn't. It's just some marketing specialists, some agents who might be looking to sign some contracts with a talented artist or two. If they don't like what they see, no one will even know that they're more than just a random guest who came to visit the gallery."

Stella sighed in relief, mentally scolding herself for having thought so negatively of Angela. The woman had been nothing but good to her, even if her business practices were less than agreeable, and it wasn't as if she were running some kind of art heist. They disagreed about how things should be done, but that didn't make her a villain. Immediately, she felt guilty for having assumed the worst when she'd gone out of her way to do something so kind for her and her students.

"Thank you. I really appreciate it, and I know my students will, too. I hope you won't mind that I don't tell them that anyone special is coming. I don't want them to feel pressured to deliver, or like they failed if they don't get signed."

"I wouldn't have it any other way. People are usually at their best when they don't know they're being head-hunted, anyway. Those artistic types prefer for everything to be organic. They hate to think anything might be forced."

Stella laughed a little. "Yeah, I get that. Thank you. Will I see you at the exhibit?"

"Actually, I think I'll be out of town, but I'm sending my love. I know you'll do great!"

With that, Angela hung up the phone. There was something in her tone that made Stella think that there might be a little more to Angela's involvement than she was letting on. Those comments about her acting skills, could they have been about how she'd departed in Seattle? Or did she know something about Stella's past that she wasn't telling her?

When the night of the exhibit rolled around, Stella was feeling more nervous than she'd ever felt before her own events. There was so much riding on this, she thought. Her students would be devastated if this didn't go perfectly, and she would never forgive herself if she made them feel like they had done something wrong. The last thing she wanted to do was discourage them from their dreams.

Truth be told, she hadn't been as hands-off as she'd promised to be. Every move they had made had been double-checked by Stella, and several decisions had been overridden. Their choice of catering had been a local pizza and wing restaurant, which was a great idea in theory, since the restaurant was popular and would certainly draw people in with the promise of free food. However, it would be difficult for people to eat, not to mention messy. Greasy hands and expensive art weren't a wonderful combination, and not all finger foods were created equal. She'd called the restaurant to cancel the order and had told her students that it had been due to a mix-up in the schedule.

"They'd already agreed to do a birthday party for a ten-year-old kid," she'd said, hoping that they wouldn't argue if she pulled at their heartstrings. She really hoped that they wouldn't question why a child would be having a party that late in the evening, nor why she didn't offer to just go pick up the food and bring it to the gallery. She was in luck, since no one seemed to push the issue. With a little bit of coercion, Stella managed to point them in the direction of catering from one of the restaurants she'd ordered from in the past, one that served more appropriate finger foods and cheap champagne.

After the food incident was subverted, she had another problem to tackle, which was flyers. They hadn't known where to hang them, so she went around after hours and asked coffee shops and libraries to ask them to put them up on their bulletin boards. These were all things she'd had to learn the hard way, by scrambling to finish them all at her first event. It seemed like so long ago now, even though it hadn't even been two years.

When Stella returned home late the Thursday night before the gallery, Kelsey was sitting at the table eating chips straight from the bag, a habit that always made Stella cringe as she watched her lick salt from her fingers and stick them back into the bag.

"What are you still doing up?"

Kelsey shrugged. "My first class is canceled tomorrow. The professor is at a lecture in the Galapagos all weekend, so I don't have to go in until, like, ten a.m."

"Well, that's nice. You could use the extra sleep."

"So could you, from the looks of it. How much running around have you been doing for this thing?"

"Enough," Stella admitted. "I'll be glad when it's over, that's for sure. I have to put a limit on these exhibits. They're so draining."

"Well, everybody is really excited about it, if that's any consolation. Joey and Dani told me."

"I'm just hoping everything goes well. I feel so guilty

about not having done as much work for this one as I have in the past."

Kelsey smirked. "Are you sure about that?" When Stella could only groan, she relaxed a bit. "Marco wants to know what to wear to this. He felt underdressed last time."

"He *was* underdressed last time."

"So, what? Slacks and a dress shirt? Will that be okay?"

Stella smiled. "Yes. And, for the record, I didn't care that he came in jeans and a t-shirt to the first exhibit. I was just flattered that he came at all. He must really care about you, because he certainly wasn't there for the art."

Kelsey laughed. "Yeah, he's a little like me that way. No real eye for it. He's more of a programmer than an artist, but he tried. He says he knows how much you mean to me, so he wants to get on your good side."

Stella felt her heart warm. "He's saying all the right things."

Truth be told, Stella didn't have any ill feelings about her daughter's boyfriend, not at all. In fact, if they were moving a little slower, she might have even felt herself coming around to liking him, as crazy as it may have sounded. He'd more than made up for his bad first impression by showing that he was crazy about Kelsey, enough to want to get close with Stella just to gain her approval. Kelsey wouldn't have confessed to caring about Stella's opinion in a million years, so he must be perceptive, too, she thought. Above all else, he truly cared about Kelsey. When she'd had to stay home from school a few weeks ago with terrible cramps, he'd not only brought her homework to her, but chocolate and a pair of warm, fuzzy socks he'd bought at a convenience store, too. He was thoughtful, and he wanted to do whatever he could for Kelsey. After everything that had happened with her father, Kelsey could use a man in her life like that.

"I'm really proud of you, Mom. I don't think you ever would have taken this chance on yourself in our old town. Something about this place makes you bold. I like it."

"Necessity," Stella joked, if only to keep herself from tearing up. "This was the only thing I knew how to do, and I had to make it work."

Kelsey wasn't about to push forward with more compliments, so she simply folded up her bag of chips to take into the bedroom with her. "I'm going to sleep. You should do the same. Tomorrow is going to be fine, okay? Don't worry."

"Goodnight, sweetheart. Love you." Kelsey muttered a, "love you, too," under her breath and Stella briefly considered ignoring her advice, but the pull of sleep at her eyelids warned her against it, so she decided to brush her teeth and hop in bed.

The following evening, Stella arrived several hours early to the exhibit, wanting to beat even her most excited students to the punch. She knew that Carrie in particular was an early bird and wasn't above waiting in her car in the parking lot for Stella to open the door, so she figured she would get a head start on setting up before that happened.

This was becoming routine to her. She skillfully set up all the spare chairs that she'd purchased for her first exhibit, making sure to space them out all over the room. She wanted to encourage folks to take their time with each piece. Her students deserved that. Honestly, she wouldn't have agreed to this if she didn't think they were ready to be seen by the general public. Each and every one of her students were incredibly talented, and she often felt the old cliché that they taught her as much as she taught them. Many of them had given her a new perspective that she hadn't previously considered, particularly those who had lived in Sunrise Beach all their lives. There was a rich inner world here, one that she was equal parts at home with and completely new to. This place never ceased to surprise her.

As for the actual setup, she barely had to lift a finger. Tim was more than happy to help the caterers set up, though Stella didn't miss the fact that he was sneaking snacks as he did so. When he noticed her watching, he looked pointedly away, but she simply smiled. This was their night, after all. She wasn't about to ruin it with a petty issue like eating the food meant for the guests. In fact, she was about to swipe an early glass of champagne for herself when the doorbell rang, too early to be a visitor but too late to be anyone involved with the setup, and she looked up in shock.

"Angela?" she asked, gaping. "I thought you were out of town."

"I was," she admitted, "but I came back. This is important."

"You didn't have to do that. We're doing fine; right, everyone?"

In the months she'd been hanging out with Angela, the star-struck awe had worn off of Stella's relationship with her, but her students had not had the same exposure, so when she looked over at them, each of them were staring in wide-eyed disbelief.

"Stella," Tim said, forcing calm into his voice that he definitely wasn't feeling, "we knew you were friends with Angela Goff, but why didn't you tell us she was going to *be* here tonight?"

She sighed. "I didn't know. I would have given some warning if I had."

Angela looked stricken. "I'm sorry. I can leave, if I'm not welcome—"

"No, no!" Carrie rushed to say. "You're more than welcome! We're just a little awestruck. I mean, to have someone so famous here... It's kind of unbelievable."

"I mean, Stella is shaping up to be a pretty big name, herself, right?" Angela said. "I've heard she had an exhibit with a celebrity."

She was referring to herself, of course, but it still made her students giddy. Though Stella half expected her to spill the beans and tell them all about the guests she'd invited, she surprisingly, blessedly, didn't.

"Angela, can I talk to you for a minute?" Angela followed Stella to one corner of the gallery and leaned in so she could hear, trying not to draw the attention of the students. "I really appreciate you coming in for this, but can I ask what happened? What changed?"

"Nothing. I just felt terrible about how we left things, and I wanted to be the one to make the first move."

"How we left things?" Stella asked, deciding it was safest to play dumb so she could have deniability. Besides, it was a reasonable question given that Angela had seemed pretty normal since they'd returned from Seattle. They hadn't fought, hadn't even brought up anything from the trip. As far as Stella was concerned, their friendship hadn't changed on Angela's side of things. Was she wrong?

"I could see that you took issue with how I handled my business in Seattle. I'm not stupid, Stella, and you're a terrible liar."

"Then why would you let me lie? Why would you pay for my airfare after I lied to you?"

She shrugged. "Like I said, the trip was all expenses paid. I wasn't going to drag you all the way across the country and then make you pay your way back. Plus, I didn't want a big fight."

"Me neither," Stella admitted. "I don't like how we left things, either. And I'm sorry for sneaking around. I just wasn't comfortable with the situation, and I didn't want you to think I was going to go home and tell or something like that."

"Oh, if I'd suspected that, I never would have brought you with me! I honestly was expecting the reaction I got, save for the fleeing. When I saw a deal like this for the first time, it made my stomach hurt, too. I'm not going to tell you how to run your art business. I've found that this is what's necessary to stay afloat, but it's your choice. It always will be."

Despite not being much of a hugger, Stella found herself leaning in when Angela threw her arms around her. Nothing was being forced on her, and she didn't have to agree with all of Angela's choices to remain friends. She had a lot of friends she didn't see eye to eye with on every issue, and she didn't cut them out of her life completely. Recognizing that it had been fear of repeating her past, not revulsion at her choices, that had turned her away from

Making Big Decisions

Angela after watching the deal go down, she decided that it was time to forgive and forget.

"Thank you for coming. I'm really glad that you're here. It just didn't feel right without you." And it hadn't. Stella wanted her friend here, wanted her mentor to see her pride and joy: her talented students in action.

By the time the event was over and everyone had filed out, leaving nothing but trash cans full of empty plates, a few cold leftovers, and a handful of unsold paintings on the walls, Stella was exhausted. She never grew used to this part of it, and even though her students had admittedly done a lot of the footwork this time, she didn't feel any less tired. The only thing that was currently getting her through the evening, not counting the two cups of coffee she'd downed before noon and three liberally-measured glasses of cheap champagne, was the fact that she'd seen several business cards exchange hands throughout the course of the night between bigwigs in the art industry and her students. Since not everyone had been handed such an opportunity, no one was talking about it, but it was still clear to Stella that a handful of them were positively glowing with a pride beyond just a successful event. Tim in particular, with his terrible poker face and whopping three business cards full of contact information for various marketing executives and talent agents, was nearly giddy.

"I can't believe how happy you've made them," Stella said to Angela. "I was really nervous about letting professionals into this space, but you were right. They were nothing but supportive."

"I wouldn't go inviting critical jerks to an event like this, Stella. I've been around the block. I remember what it was like to have my work ripped into when I wasn't expecting it, and it was awful. The last thing I want to do is put anybody through that."

Stella nodded. "I'm sorry for doubting you." Though she couldn't say it aloud, she didn't just mean about the guests. She was apologizing for jumping to conclusions, for judging her so harshly when she really didn't know what it took to operate a business like Angela's. From now on, she vowed to assume the best about her friend while still keeping her at an arm's length from her gallery and classes. Angela had proven herself a loyal enough friend to deserve that much from her.

Chapter Fifteen

Stella wasn't terribly happy about the fact that Marco took Kelsey to his own apartment after the exhibit, but she bit her tongue when she saw her the next morning. Marco was still driving Kelsey to school every morning and had recently moved to be closer to campus, which meant that he was having to go almost twenty minutes out of his way every morning just to pick Kelsey up for school. When they'd first moved, Stella had been able to allow Kelsey to drive herself, or at least had been able to drop her off on days where she needed the car, but now, her business was too demanding for that. Kelsey had her own schedule and was often out either studying, hanging with her friends, or working at her internship until late at night, and Stella used the car nearly every day now that she was teaching at the college. Between her classes there and having to buy supplies for her own studio, allowing Kelsey to use the car to get to and from class wasn't really an option. It meant that unless she wanted to demand that Marco drive almost an hour more a day just to transport her daughter back and forth, she had to think of an alternative.

Unfortunately, Kelsey beat her to the punch by asking if she could start staying over at Marco's new apartment during the week.

"Absolutely not," Stella had said, a knee-jerk reaction that had made Kelsey immediately defensive.

"Come on, Mom. You can't expect him to drive all the way out here every day just to pick me up."

"What about Mariah? Can't you hitch a ride with her like you were doing last semester?"

"She got a job at a café and works in the mornings. Her classes don't start until noon every day this semester, since she picked the latest ones she could find."

Stella was undeterred. "Well, you have lots of other friends who could give you rides, right? What about Dani and Joey?"

"They live on the total other end of town. It's either this, or I have to get a car. I'm not trying to be difficult. Those are just the only two options that make sense, don't you think?"

She hated that she agreed, but Kelsey had a point. She couldn't expect her friends to go so far out of their way for her, and they simply didn't have the money for a new car right now. Their old, half-broken-down one already gave them enough trouble.

"There are going to be rules."

Kelsey looked up in surprise, clearly not having expected this to happen without more of a fight. Truthfully, Stella just didn't want to fight Kelsey on much, these days. She was a grown woman who was ready to make her own choices, and she'd shown a lot of maturity in the past years, especially given the circumstances.

"Right. I'm not asking to move in with him or anything," she quickly promised. "I just think it makes sense to stay there during the week. Sunday through Friday."

"Friday after school, Marco drops you here. He can stick around, if he wants, but I want to see you. I would say also that your grades can't suffer, but I know you would never let that happen. Your internship, though, and your sleep schedule need to be a priority, too. I don't want you staying up late watching TV with your boyfriend every night."

If she expected a fight, she would have been wrong. Kelsey simply nodded gratefully, demonstrating just the kind of maturity that was a major factor in Stella being able to make this sort of decision. It was true that she didn't love the idea of her daughter living in sin, but she also knew that this generation was different from her own, and besides, she had technically done the same thing, albeit under different circumstances. Kids these days were living together to ensure that they wanted to get married down the line rather than going in the opposite order. Though it would have made her mother break out in hives to think about, Stella knew that she had to let Kelsey decide this for herself. Anything that kept her from rushing into marriage was a positive, anyway.

"I'll text you every night before I go to bed so you know I'm safe, and I can send one when I get to school, too, if it helps. I'll still be at all your art events, and I'll live with you over my breaks. This is just so much closer to my internship, and it'll be way easier for Marco to drive me to school."

"I'll miss you like crazy."

To Stella's surprise, Kelsey looked a little misty-eyed. "I'll miss you, too, Mom." Letting them grow up was the hardest part of parenting, she decided at this moment. Every sleepless night of reverse cycling, the hours of screaming when Kelsey had been teething, the screaming matches she'd instigated when she'd been an angry teenager—none of it compared to this. Even before Kelsey began to pack, the house was feeling emptier than it ever had before.

Even though Kelsey wasn't moving out for good, packing was almost as much work as if she had been. She had to take most of her clothes, considering she would be out of the house five out of seven days a week. Her electronics, both those she needed for school and the ones that were just for fun, went with her, as well as shower supplies, schoolbooks, and a supply of food massive enough to sustain both of the kids for a month. Stella had taken one look at Marco's pantry and decided she would buy fresh vegetables and healthy snacks, since he had mostly instant noodles and frozen pizza rolls in the kitchen. Kelsey wasn't into cooking, but hopefully, she would learn. In addition to that, Stella cooked and froze a few nutritious meals in case she was feeling lazy or tired.

On the first night Kelsey officially stayed with Marco, Stella was a wreck. The entire day had been busy, full of moving and unpacking Kelsey's boxes into Marco's apartment. He'd been a good sport about it, never questioning why she needed to stock their bathroom with makeup if she hardly even wore it or keep so many pairs of shoes in the closet if she really only ever alternated between sneakers and boots. He lifted the heaviest boxes, those full of books and technology, and had the good sense to leave her clothes untouched. He had even cleared out over half of his closet to give her space, which Stella appreciated. He was trying to make her feel at home, which was the most important thing.

Kelsey had never lived away from her mother before. As a child, she hated sleepovers. Almost invariably, she would call Stella at some ungodly hour of the night, crying and begging to be picked up because she couldn't sleep anywhere but her own bed.

When they had moved to Sunrise Beach, it had been an adjustment for her. After all, they had moved into their big house when Kelsey was pretty young and had remained there ever since, so it had been a long time since she'd occupied any room other than her own. When the IRS had chased them out of the house, she hadn't really had time to grab much in the way of her room decorations, so all her fairy lights and posters had been left behind. The walls of her new room had remained, despite Stella's encouragement to go out and buy anything she wanted, stubbornly unadorned.

They had gone out that Saturday morning to get coffee, something they rarely did since Stella thought it was an unnecessary expense, as she could brew it at home. The line for the local café was short, as most of the sleepy beachside town slept in on Saturdays, so they'd ordered pastries and coffee: Stella's black, and Kelsey's iced and overly sweet.

"How are you feeling about the idea of living with Marco during the week?" Stella asked. She expected idealistic optimism, but Kelsey once again surprised her.

"I'm a little nervous. I mean, I've never lived with a boy. I didn't even grow up with siblings, you know? What if I hate having to share my space with someone else?"

Stella shrugged. She could use the opportunity, she realized, to persuade her to stay, but she didn't. "Everyone does, at first. It's an adjustment. You just have to set boundaries. Make sure you both have drawers of things that are only yours, and spaces where you can go to get some alone time, if you need it. No matter how much you like someone, it's hard to be with them twenty-four seven."

"I'm so worried about that."

"About not liking to be with him?"

"No," she admitted. "About him not liking to be with me."

"Kelsey, you are sweet, fun, smart, and wonderful. He's lucky to have you moving in."

"What if I'm obnoxious to live with?"

"Then you two talk about it and work through it. You know, when your father and I started living together on our own, he had no idea how to run the washer. I mean, it was comical. His mother had done his laundry his entire life, and it was like he thought the washer was some magical device that sucked your clothes up off the floor and returned them to your drawers clean and folded. It drove me nuts."

"How did you fix it?"

Stella frowned. "I told him that if he didn't pick up his clothes, I was going to donate them all to Goodwill."

"And?"

"He picked them up. That night, he called Grandma Gwen and asked how to do his laundry. It was a little pathetic, but he never left his dirty clothes on the floor again, and I realized that what made me so mad wasn't that his dirty clothes were on the floor, but that he wasn't respecting me enough to pick them up. When he called his mom to learn how to wash them, it showed me that he did care, and it meant so much. I only hope that Marco shows you that same kind of respect."

It wasn't as if she wanted Kelsey to find a man like her father, but they'd always made it a point to model healthy relationships for her. Or, at least, they'd tried. The lying and betrayal and heartbreak had undone a lot of that. Still, when things had been good, they'd been very good. If Marco treated Kelsey anything like Jeff had treated her in the beginning, she would be happy,

"Did you hear that it's, like, the hottest day of the year today?"

"Great. Marco's building has an elevator, right?" she asked, knowing better than to hope and finding her suspicions confirmed when Kelsey shook her head.

Chapter Sixteen

The house was quiet without Kelsey. Somehow, even though she spent all her time in her room with her headphones in, often so silent that Stella could forget she was even home, her absence was overwhelming.

Stella tried to keep herself busy, first with chores. That kept her occupied for longer than she'd like to admit, a long list having piled up in the wake of the exhibit. It had been far too much time since she'd vacuumed, swept, or changed her sheets. After the bare bones were done, she shifted to wiping down the baseboards, dusting the ceiling fans, and removing the spiderwebs from all the windows. She washed the car by hand, something she never wasted time doing unless she had too much of it to spare, and detailed the interior. By the end of the first week, her house was sparkling.

After the cleaning spree, she found herself less antsy and more bored. She had no one to cook for, so her simple meals became even more lazy. Often, she just toasted a bagel or ate a bowl of cold cereal over the sink. She promised herself she wouldn't get takeout every night, but that was hit or miss so far.

Felicia called often, and they began spending more time together. Once a week, they went to a half price movie at the theater, which was usually terrible. Stella even began to branch out and hang out with some of the women in town she had never really gotten to know. She began bowling every other week with Jessica, the daughter of the man from whom she rented her gallery, and a few of Jessica's sisters. Apparently she had six of them; who knew? Mr. and Mrs. Jeong, with whom she shared her building strip, had her over for dinner a time or two, which she loved, since Mrs. Jeong was an incredible cook. Even a few of the other teachers at the college invited her out to the local pub every Friday, and she dropped in every now and again to have a drink and chat with her coworkers, reveling in how strange it was to have those for the first time in decades.

Kelsey stayed true to her word and either called or texted every night to prove that she was alive and well. Which is why when Stella's phone rang first thing in the morning, she was a bit confused as to why Kelsey was even awake, though she didn't bother to spare a glance at her phone before picking it up.

"Hey, early bird," she greeted, and a warm, deep voice on the other end of the line chuckled.

"It's actually almost noon here," said Grant. Grant Townsend, Felicia's handsome older brother, the man with whom Stella had shared a weeks-long summer romance and two wonderful kisses before the relationship had ended in an argument—with him leaving to go back to the UK—was calling her. She hadn't heard from him directly in months, though Felicia told her often that he was doing well and gave her updates on what he was up to. Though she tried to convince herself that she didn't care, she knew that she was lying to herself, just as she was lying to herself when she forced herself to believe she was anything but thrilled to hear his voice.

"Grant," she breathed, too shocked to say much else. "Wow."

"Yeah. How have you been doing, Stella?"

She laughed. "Oh, you know. Same old, same old. What about you?"

"Similar, though knowing you, I find that difficult to believe. Felicia told me about your newest exhibits. I've heard you've done one with a very famous artist. Even I'd heard of Angela Goff, and I'm about as far removed from the arts as one can get."

She couldn't help but laugh at that. "She reached out to me and asked me to do an exhibit with her, and I wasn't about to say no. It was honestly pretty surreal. Still is, if I'm being honest."

Suddenly, Stella felt the urge to tell him everything that had happened over the time he'd been gone, from the exhibit with Angela to the disastrous trip to Seattle, but she refrained. The last time they'd spoken, Graham had crossed a line. He'd joked about something he had no business talking about, and to make it worse, it was in front of an important art critic. He had known just how sensitive she was about people finding out the circumstances of her divorce, namely the crimes that Jeff had committed, and he'd made light of that. Time had taken the heat out of the anger, but it hadn't yet been replaced by trust. This was like hearing from an old friend, she told herself, nothing more. She had to be guarded, measured in what she said to him.

"Well, in any case, I'm sure it was incredible to behold. I'm just sorry I couldn't have been there to watch you work. The few times I got to see you shine were all a privilege, and I'm sure that Angela knew how to bring out that spark in you."

She felt her cheeks heat up and was grateful that this was just a voice call and not a video chat.

"I'm not trying to be rude, but what made you decide you wanted to call me after so long? It's been months, Graham. Honestly, I was beginning to wonder if I'd ever hear from you again."

"If you want the truth," he said, "it's not that I suddenly decided I wanted to call. I've wanted to since the minute my plane landed in Manchester, but Felicia discouraged it. She said you were still upset and that I needed to give you space, so I was trying to do that."

"And she's telling you something different now?"

He sighed. "No. I just couldn't wait any longer, and I figured that you were the best person to ask whether or not you were still angry with me." He paused, waiting for her to confirm or deny... and spoke again when she did neither. "So? Are you? Angry with me, that is."

Stella let him squirm for a a long moment, enjoying having him in such a vulnerable position, before smiling. "No, Graham. I'm not. I was upset, and I felt hurt and betrayed by what happened, but I'm not angry. I'm over it."

He loudly let out a breath that Stella hadn't realized he'd been holding. "Oh, thank goodness. I'd have felt a right sod if you'd said yes and hung up."

She laughed. "I'm not hanging up. Actually, it's great to hear from you. Kelsey moved out recently, so the house has been pretty empty lately. Any companionship is welcome, really."

He gasped. "No way, she did? I can't believe that. She seems so young. I'm surprised you let her."

"Well, she's not properly moved out, just staying with her boyfriend during the week to be closer to school, but still. It's been lonely."

"I can only imagine. That's crazy. How is she enjoying it?"

"Oh, Kelsey loves it. It's me who's losing my mind. I don't love her living with her boyfriend."

Graham laughed, a sound that Stella had to admit she'd missed. "I imagine you don't. But hey... it's so good to hear your voice. I really hated how we left things. I was worried you weren't going to pick up the phone when I called."

"I thought you were Kelsey."

"I'll take a win however I can get it."

Stella smiled. "If it's any consolation, I'm glad I did pick up."

From there, the two talked on the phone for almost an hour. Graham told Stella all about his job, how boring he found it and how much he missed the States. He wanted nothing more than to come back to Sunrise Beach and see her and Felicia again, or so he said, but work was tying him to Europe for the foreseeable future. He was doing a lot of local traveling, which he was enjoying, and for a brief moment, Stella allowed herself to wonder what her life might look like if she were with him on those trips. Eating in warm French cafés, walking through little gardens in

Germany, painting the cobblestone streets of London. All of it sounded appealing to Stella. Someday, she promised herself she would visit. She would make Graham show her around all the best spots for painting and take her to the best restaurants. After Kelsey graduated, maybe, she told him. Graham said that he was looking forward to it in a way that implied he didn't believe it would ever really happen—*but she would show him*. She would be unpredictable, would someday do things just for herself. Just not today.

Stella had to admit that the way she felt chatting on the phone with Graham was more than just catching up with an old friend. It didn't quite spark the fireworks she'd experienced the first time they'd met, or on their dates, but she found herself coming up with excuses not to hang up each time there was a natural lull that could serve as a way out. As much as she tried to deny it, she still had feelings for Graham. She was sure he had them for her, too. His laughter was so warm when she cracked jokes, asked questions about her art and her life that kept her talking more than listening, something she wasn't used to. Normally, Stella was the one asking questions, keeping her own personal life close to the chest. Graham knew it all, so she could open up to him in a way she couldn't with others. She even told him about the letters that Jeff had written to her, which piqued his interest more than she'd expected.

"He wrote to you? Wow. I assume you burned the letter?"

Stella laughed. "I thought about it," she admitted, "but no. At first, I just kept it in a drawer, but he kept writing, and the guilt kept building. I thought I might throw them away, but I had a moment of tenderness, I guess. I don't know why, but I decided to write back."

"No way! I'd have thought you would tell him to get lost."

"Believe me, I wanted to," she chucked. "But then I thought, he loves Kelsey. If I'd made a horrible choice and made Jeff never want to speak to me again, I would at least hope that he would let me know how my daughter was doing. I know his mother tells him, but I imagine it's not the same. I would want to hear it from the person who lives with her."

"That's very mature of you. I can't say I would have the strength to do the same, after what he did."

Stella hadn't thought much of her decision to write Jeff back, honestly. It had just felt like the right thing to do, the only thing to do. She had asked herself if she thought he would do the same for her if the roles were reversed, and when she couldn't come up with an answer, she decided to ask herself instead if she hoped that he would. Unequivocally, indisputably, the answer had been yes. Nothing in the world could have kept her from wanting to hear from her daughter, and if Kelsey didn't want to talk to him, the least she could do was make sure that she herself kept up correspondence. There were no laws that stated that a parent had to bring their child to see an incarcerated parent, even though Kelsey had only been fifteen when he had gone to jail. Stella had checked to make sure of that. When Jeff had been arrested, she'd left it up to Kelsey whether she wanted to visit, and she hadn't. As much as what he'd done hurt Stella, it had damaged Kelsey even more.

"Well, in any case, it's not like we're actually corresponding. He never replied to my letter, since I don't think I really gave the indication that I wanted to hear from him again. Hopefully, he's satisfied now and will leave us alone."

If that was what she wanted, she shouldn't have encouraged him, she chastised herself, but she tried not to dwell on that. Instead, she allowed herself to be wrapped up in how nice it was to catch up with this other man she had thought she wouldn't ever hear from again, whom she'd told herself she hadn't wanted to hear from. It was nice, she had to admit. It made her feel less lonely.

"You know, if Kelsey is going to be out of the house more often, I could start calling more frequently. I know I'm five hours ahead of where you are, but I'm sure we could find a schedule that works for both of us, if you were interested."

Was she interested? Was this what she wanted? How long had it been since she'd actually asked herself what she wanted?

"We'll take it slow," she finally decided. "Next time, I'll call you."

After hanging up with Graham for the afternoon, Stella thought to herself it was probably better that she hadn't moved to Seattle, after all. If Graham were to visit anywhere in the United States, it would be here, where his sister lived. And what she knew for sure was that the next time he was in town, however far in the future that might be, she wanted to see him. Talking on the phone had rekindled the spark between them, and though it wasn't anything so finite or dramatic as a full-blown desire for a relationship, she couldn't deny the parts of her that wanted to see him again. Besides, everything she had told him about how she'd been doing since he'd left, had centered on Sunrise Beach. Sure, she'd had a wild adventure on the other side of the country, but it had been forgettable, save for a few unsavory parts that were a little more difficult to let go of. Most of what she'd wanted to tell him about was all the wonders of her life right here, in the life she'd built for herself.

Chapter Seventeen

The first weekend that Kelsey came home had Stella feeling more excited than she had in a long time. She'd been so bored, and though she was able to fill her days with work and friends, she missed having someone to talk to at night. Stella had originally planned to make something special for Kelsey for dinner, but decided against it. There was nothing Stella could make that Kelsey would enjoy eating more than Thai food from her favorite takeout place downtown, which she rarely went to because it was so far out of the way, so Stella paid the extra few bucks to have it delivered.

When Kelsey came in through the door with Marco trailing close behind, Stella couldn't deny that she felt a little disappointed. She'd hoped that she would see Kelsey alone, but she couldn't complain, since she had told her that Marco was allowed over to her place on Fridays.

"Hey, you two," she greeted. "Dinner is on its way. I only ordered two entrees, but this place's portions give you enough for two people each. Do you like Thai, Marco?"

Kelsey shook her head. "He's not staying. Not for dinner, anyway."

"Yeah, sorry about that," he said sheepishly. "I'm having dinner with an old friend who came to town."

Kelsey's fake smile implied that she wasn't happy about it, so Stella guessed it was a female friend from childhood, perhaps one that she'd heard stories about.

"Well, that will be fun. You didn't want to go, honey?"

Kelsey shrugged. "She was invited," Marco said, defending himself.

"I just wanted to eat here. With you."

Though she now knew that this was likely a decision made more from petty jealousy than real desire to have dinner with her, Stella vowed to make the evening worth it for her. "Well, we'll have a good time. We can rent a movie, eat dinner. Maybe we'll even go get milkshakes, if you want."

Kelsey made a point to look thrilled, more so than she probably felt. "Sounds perfect. I'll see you Monday, Marco."

He took his cue to leave, and Stella smiled. "Want to pick a movie?"

Over dinner, Kelsey didn't want to talk about Marco. In fact, she avoided the subject like the plague, even when Stella tried to direct the conversation that way. As much as she hated to defend the boyfriend over her daughter, she remembered being nineteen years old and jealous, and she looked back on those memories now and laughed at how ridiculous it all had been. She'd felt envious whenever Jeff spent time with female friends, even those she knew he had no romantic interest in. It was an insecure time in development, and Kelsey was right in the worst of it.

"How was your first week staying over at Marco's?" she asked after less direct approaches failed.

She shrugged. "It was good, I guess. I mostly just studied. Not so different from living here."

"I'm not sure if that's a good or a bad thing, but I'm glad it hasn't been too jarring, at least. I was worried that you were going to struggle to focus, sharing a room with your boyfriend."

"Nah," Kelsey dismissed around a bite of khao pad. "Marco leaves me alone for the most part. He studies a lot, too, so we usually just turn on something stupid on the TV and half watch it while we study in the living room. It's kind of nice, actually. I feel like it keeps me focused, since I've got someone there who would know if I got distracted and started messing around."

Stella smiled. "Like you used to. You know, when you did your homework in the living room while we watched. Dad used to get so annoyed because I wouldn't let him watch football while you were studying."

"Oh, man. I must have been really young. I barely even remember that."

"You did it all the time. I got so sad when you turned eleven and decided you wanted to do your homework in your room, but Dad couldn't have been happier to buy you a desk."

The wave of nostalgia was intense as it washed over Stella, reminding her of all the things she'd had at one point in her past. At that time, everything had just fallen into place. She hadn't had to force it, hadn't even really had to work at it. Sure, raising a child wasn't easy, and her and Jeff's marriage wasn't perfect even before his arrest, but things had felt, at that time, natural. She'd never had to think about her next step forward, as it had always been clear. She was living with her boyfriend, so the only decision that made sense was to get married. They were married and living together, so the next logical step was to have a child. Everything had just made sense, until it hadn't. Then, nothing made sense.

As if she were thinking the same thing, Kelsey sighed. "You know, as many good memories I have of home, I think we're really in a better place now. Both literally and figuratively. I love it here, and I've never seen you happier. I know you're working really hard, but the stuff you're accomplishing is just amazing."

"I think you're right," Stella agreed. However, there was still another thought nagging at her. "Do you think this is it for us?"

"What do you mean?"

"I don't know. Just, it feels like everything got a lot better for us when we made this one drastic change, and now we've been settled here for a while, and it's wonderful, but... I guess I sometimes wonder if this is all there is, or if there's something more waiting for us. Or for me."

"What more do you want?" Kelsey asked. There was no hint of animosity in her tone, nor of judgment, just curiosity. "Your art career is thriving, you're teaching classes on your own and at the college. I mean, I'm sure you miss your new boyfriend, but—"

"Oh, stop," Stella admonished playfully, slapping her on the arm lightly. "It's not about a guy. I'm not even sure what I mean, really. I got a taste of how wide the world is, maybe, and I just want to drink it all up."

"Seattle really treated you well, huh?"

"Not even a little," she laughed. "Forget I said anything. Come on, we should start *Moulin Rouge* soon if we want to finish it before bedtime."

Though she loved that movie, Stella couldn't focus on it. Her thoughts were drawn once more to the vague idea that she was still missing out, like there was something more waiting for her that she didn't yet know how to achieve. After all, when her life was ideal and she'd wanted for nothing, she'd stayed stagnant. It wasn't until she'd been forced to provide for herself and Kelsey that she'd had to dig deep and make things happen. That had been the catalyst for everything else. Now that she was stable again, happy again, would that all stop? Was she now at her peak solely because she was comfortable?

That night, with Kelsey in her room likely winding down to go to sleep, Stella headed silently into her studio to paint. It was not only rare for her to paint in her home studio these days, but she certainly almost never painted at night. She was, by nature, a morning person, which inevitably meant that she was early to bed, too, but tonight, this idea was gripping her. Kelsey liked to take walks after dinner. A friend of hers years ago had told her that in Korean culture, it was believed that walking aided digestion, and that some science later backed the old wives tale. Ever since then, whenever she ate something spicy or acidic, or if she wanted a late dinner, she tried to get a short walk in after the meal. Normally, she insisted on doing this alone, but tonight, she'd invited Stella along with her, which had given her a glimpse of a view she didn't often see, which was the beach in the evening.

A mother rarely sees sunsets, Stella thought. For years, she'd spent the hour or so after dinner cleaning up the kitchen and putting away leftovers, and by the time she was done, the sun had usually gone down. Seeing a sunset was special to her, especially on a night when she'd eaten a meal with Kelsey rather than just grabbing a bowl of cold cereal by herself and sticking the plate in the dishwasher. Her evenings were usually spent either cleaning or working on things for her art studio, but having a child made her slow down every once in a while and just enjoy things. Tonight was one of those nights.

As they had walked, Kelsey took her down to the docks. They were near the beach but far removed from the areas that were packed full of people; Kelsey said that having to deal with a crowd ruined the relaxation that was supposed to help her digest. The docks were where the fishermen stood in the early mornings to get seafood for local restaurants, but now, in the late evening after the workday had ended, they were quiet. The only light came from the sliver of the sun that hadn't yet ducked below the waves, and the streetlights that were beginning to illuminate for the evening. It wasn't just the fact that the sunset was beautiful, which it was, but the fact that Stella felt so wonderful looking at it that made her want to paint it. She wasn't trying to be cliché with her subjects, but she supposed that some things were best enjoyed in the darkness, and this segment of the beach was one of them. She'd painted it so many times before, but never like this. It matched her mindset: the dark, cloudy night that was so easily and beautifully lit from just the smallest bit of light. The evening held desperately to the sun even as it set, and even once it was no longer visible, a thick halo of light could be seen above the water.

When she hung the painting on her wall a week from that night, once the thick layers of oil paint were nice and dry, she was a little afraid that it would look strange sitting with the rest of her works. She'd painted a lot of sunrises, and a few early-evening sunsets, but never one like this, in the last moments of dusk. Against the rest of her art, this one was dark, but she found that she didn't care much whether or not it sold. She was proud of it, and that was what mattered.

As with most of her paintings, particularly the ones where she had felt like she was taking a risk, she was shocked at the response. For the first few days, it got a lot of attention. People who hadn't purchased a piece in months were stopping in front of it and gazing, lost in the nighttime beauty of their town. That was one thing she loved about watching people enjoy her art—most of them lived here, so she felt like she was giving them a love letter to the town they already loved so much. It was just a small thing she was able to give back to the place that had been there for her after her divorce, a small bit of appreciation. The beach deserved that amount of detail, of love. She would love nothing more than for her art to draw people in to visit Sunrise Beach.

Her regulars weren't the only people who were enjoying it, though. A week and a half after hanging it in the gallery, no one had yet made an offer on the painting even though several people had expressed interest. She was beginning to wonder if this one was going to flop, after all, when a man she recognized strolled into her shop.

"Andrew?" she called in disbelief. "Andrew Johnson?"

The man grinned, turning to her with excitement in his eyes. "Stella! I was hoping you'd be in today. I know your hours have changed, since you were offering so many classes. Angela told me you were even teaching at some college now."

He made no effort to disguise the displeasure in his voice at that. Andrew was someone that Stella had been introduced to in Seattle. Luckily, he wasn't one of the shadier contacts that Angela had coerced her to meet, but she still didn't necessarily feel great about the fact that he'd showed up unannounced. Stella was doing her best to block out most of that trip from her memory.

"I'm shocked you're here. What brings you to Sunrise Beach?"

"You, of course," he said, then hesitated. "Well, I suppose that's not entirely true. You and another artist here in South Carolina. I wanted to get a look at his gallery, and yours was on the way, so I invited myself." Immediately,

Andrew's gaze was drawn across the room to the night scene she'd just painted. "What's this?"

Stella chuckled. "Oh, that was just... I don't know, a bit of a whim. I'm not sure how I feel about it yet." That wasn't true—she loved that piece, and she made a mental note to stop doing this. It was a bad habit from her days having to deal with Jeff's friends, who were often judgmental about strange things. She reserved her own opinions until she knew how it was going to be received, but that was something she needed to cease doing in her quest to be authentically, unapologetically herself. Angela was that way, and so had Adele been. None of the women she most admired would hold their tongues just to earn the favor of someone else, especially someone she didn't even like.

"It's ethereal, darling. It really is. It barely even looks like the same place you usually paint."

"It's not. I usually paint the beach, and this is the docks. The beaches are for the public and the tourists, but no one but the fishermen usually have any business hanging around the docks. My daughter and I passed through recently and there was just something alluring about the seclusion of it. The water seemed so much more still, even though it's obviously just as affected by the tides as anywhere else."

"It's almost magical. I could get lost in this painting. How much?"

Stella blinked. Though she'd been trying to sell it since she hung it up, now that it was really happening, she felt a little sad about it. Normally, she didn't get attached to her paintings solely because she would have to let them go, but this one had legs, like a good wine. It stayed with her even after she was finished painting it.

"I don't know. What do you think is fair?"

Andrew looked at her with an expression that was equal parts condescension and genuine humor. "You should probably know those things. Otherwise, it's easy to take advantage of you. What would you say if I offered you two hundred and fifty dollars for the painting right now?"

She felt her cheeks heat up. "Well, that's obviously not enough." Two years ago, that would have sounded like a dream, but things were different now. Stella wasn't a no-name little wannabe artist anymore.

He nodded. "How about if I doubled it? five hundred dollars?" She shook her head, though that wasn't a price she considered to be absurd. "And if I doubled that? A thousand?"

She bit her bottom lip. "That sounds fair. I would sell it for that price."

Andrew shook his head, clearly not satisfied with what he'd heard. "You're above that, now. You can't be selling your art for prices like that. For a piece that large, one with so many layers of oil, one I can tell took you hours if not days—you should accept no less than five thousand."

She had to consciously tell herself not to let her jaw drop when she heard that number. There was no way she could charge prices like that. She was in the middle of a little community, and most of her customers were small business owners looking to hang local art in their shops, not art collectors who wanted to brag about how much they spent on a certain collection.

"With all due respect, people don't charge prices like that in a town like this. My clientele are mostly—"

"Locals, I know. And that's exactly the problem. A place like this is only going to hold you back. I know you have some attachment to it because it's where you got your start, but everyone eventually outgrows their nest, no matter how secure and comforting it is."

Stella had not asked for this man's advice, but now that she'd listened to it, she couldn't help but wonder if maybe he was right.

"I'm happy with where I'm at and what I make. I don't need any more." It was said as much to convince herself as it was for him. On the one hand, it was true. Stella had never set out to make riches, only a comfortable living for herself and her daughter. Anything more than that, she could take or leave. She'd had astronomical amounts of money for much of her adult life, and it hadn't made her happy. Her life with Jeff and Kelsey was just as happy before the money as it was after, and when the IRS had taken it all, the most upsetting part had not been the money, but the house, her sense of stability.

Still, taking money out of the equation, it would be nice to be successful. If there were better ways to measure success in this business than by the cost of a painting, Stella wasn't sure what they were. This man, this professional in the industry, was telling her she could sell her art for a price that transcended whatever skill and popularity level she had ever imagined herself achieving.

"You rely on teaching classes as your primary source of income, don't you?" That question was asked with scorn, too, like he wouldn't be able to take her seriously as an artist if she were teaching classes. She nodded anyway, and his vindicated expression made her blood boil. "What happens if that dries up? Art teachers face both feast and famine. It's not always up to you who takes your classes."

It wasn't as if Stella hadn't ever fretted about that before, but it felt more malicious coming from Andrew. He wasn't looking out for her like Angela always had been—he was judging her talent and her choices.

"Well, I suppose I'll burn that bridge when I get to it." He laughed at that, sensing the cue in her tone to drop the subject. She tried not to take what he had said to heart as she sold him the painting.

Chapter Eighteen

As if Andrew's words were a prediction, when the semester ended and enrollment opened up again, Stella's classes were not nearly as popular as they'd been in the past. Several of the students she had expected to take the next course dropped, and in fact, by the time the sign-up period was closed, Stella's class only had two students. The department head called her into her office the very same day and Stella had a sinking feeling that she knew where this was going.

"I know that we gave you an enormous space last semester. I mean, you needed it, with all the students you had! But... Stella, I'm not sure if you've had a chance to look at the student list yet—"

"I know," she interjected, trying and failing to hide her disappointment. "It's a small class." It was barely even a class. Would they pull the plug on it altogether?

"These things happen. I just want to be realistic about how much space you need, so I was thinking of moving your class to a different room. Is that okay?"

It wasn't, not really, but Stella nodded anyway. This was exactly what she'd feared. Her class size was dwindling already, so early on in her art career. She felt like she'd barely even been teaching for any length of time and her time was already up. She had already been noticing a gradual decline in the attendance for her classes in her studio, which was why she'd been so excited to be offered a job working for the community college. A place like this wouldn't rely so much on word of mouth, and she didn't have to do any work to advertise.

"Please don't sweat this too much. Things like this... well, interest comes and goes. You know how tough the economy has been lately. A lot of folks are struggling to make ends meet, and art classes are always the first thing people think to cut out of their lives when they're trying to save money."

Stella understood that, too. That had been what had held her back from taking art classes when she was young, right after she and Jeff had moved out on their own and before he had a steady job. Both of them had just been working bussing tables at restaurants, and money had been tight. She'd experienced that again after the divorce, but once she had started making good money of her own, she hadn't thought it would affect her again. Worrying about money was one of her least favorite preoccupations. It brought up too many memories of Jeff, and sometimes, if she was feeling stressed enough about it, she could almost start to see where he was coming from and why he did what he did.

Stella thanked Merry and closed the office door behind her. She couldn't be here right now, and besides, she had another class to start preparing, even if there were only two students on the register. She headed back to her gallery so she could prepare her next curriculum while waiting for customers. Unfortunately, she had a lot of waiting time on her hands, since the sales part of her art career wasn't going much better than her classes. The recession made people scale back on purchases like original artwork, too, and as her name became known around town, it seemed, fewer people wanted to buy her art because the price was simply too high.

Was she selling herself short, she wondered, by staying here? Andrew had paid an entire month's worth of income in one fell swoop, but she couldn't possibly want that sort of life, could she? Angela had shown her exactly the kinds of sacrifices she would have to make to live that part of the dream. There was a lot underneath the pristine surface, and Stella stood firm in not wanting any part of that.

Instead, she waited for customers. While she eyed the door for hours, hoping that anyone might stop by, she planned her next classes, trying not to recycle too much from her previous classes. Neither of these students had taken her class before, but she didn't want to become known for recycling the same content over and over, since that would drastically discourage anyone from taking a second course with her.

At least, she thought, Kelsey would be back home that night. It was Friday, after all, and Kelsey was usually already waiting in the living room for her when she got home on Fridays, watching television and eating snacks. All her stress was worth it for Kelsey, so she resisted the urge to give up and close the doors early, and stuck it out until her advertised closing time, trying not to feel too disappointed that no one had walked in even after so many hours.

"Kelsey, I'm home," Stella called as she took off her shoes in the doorway. When there was no response, she rolled her eyes. Kelsey was probably in her room with her headphones on. "Kelsey!" she tried again—louder this time—but still, nothing. She walked down the hall and opened Kelsey's door only to find her bed empty, which made her heart rate start to pick up a little. Stella wasn't prone to anxiety, but when she expected to see her daughter and didn't, there was a small prickle of panic that arose despite herself.

She checked her phone, but there was nothing there. Typical. Kelsey must have decided to go home with Marco even though it was spring break and she was supposed to come home. She took out her phone and typed up a quick text explaining that she needed to know where Kelsey was. Perhaps it was worded a little aggressively, but she was her mother, and she had a right to know these things.

"Please call when you can. We agreed that you would spend your break here. Love you."

What she didn't say and perhaps should have, was that she was looking forward to Kelsey's return that evening, that she needed some cheering up after the difficult day she'd had and knew that no one could make her happier than her daughter. Now that Kelsey spent most of her time out of the house, she valued their time together even more.

She didn't anticipate that Kelsey would respond well to her text—she never did when Stella was trying to put her foot down. She was at that age where she thought she knew everything, thought she was so mature and should be allowed to make any decision she wanted. Stella knew that wasn't true, but at the same time, she also knew that Kelsey was, technically, an adult.

Then she remembered the months that they had spent barely speaking. When they'd first moved, things had been so rocky between them that Kelsey hardly wanted to say a word to her. Things had gotten so much better, and Kelsey finally trusted her again. She was sharing details of her life, talking to her, and asking for advice when she needed it. Stella weighed the cost of losing that communication against her anger at Kelsey breaking this rule, and decided that it wasn't worth it.

Now knowing that Kelsey wasn't going to be coming back that evening after all, Stella racked her brain for how she was going to fill the week. Of course, since she taught at the same school Kelsey attended, she had no classes to teach, and her personal ones weren't going to start up for another two weeks. She'd been planning her curriculums and was nearly done, but found it difficult to get motivated when she knew that so few students would attend. More than anything, she wanted to paint, but felt no inspiration. Instead, she sank into the couch and turned on a movie, hoping to fall asleep there and wake up in a better mood the next morning.

If Kelsey had come home that evening, she wouldn't have caved and agreed to go out for drinks with Angela. She'd been keeping her distance, not just because of what had happened in Seattle, but because she felt a little embarrassed about how things were going for herself. Her classes, which were the meat of her income, were dwindling, and she barely sold enough paintings to get by. If Angela offered her the same deal now, it would probably feel a lot more tempting.

Still, she was lonely, and more than that, she was bored, so when Angela asked her out to a bar that night to catch up, Stella didn't decline. Instead, she put on a nice dress, did her makeup, and drove out to meet Angela at the bar she hadn't been to since the night of their collaborative exhibit.

Stella liked this bar because it seemed to be aimed toward adults her own age. Most places played music so loudly that she couldn't have a conversation, but this one was well-lit, clean, and played their music at a reasonable volume. Kelsey would think a place like this was lame, but she enjoyed it.

"To be perfectly frank, I didn't think you'd want to come out with me," Angela admitted after their first round of drinks was delivered. "Not after Seattle."

"I overreacted. You were right. It's not like you were asking me to do some kind of illicit deal. I shouldn't have freaked out and left. Plus, after everything you did to get those talent agents to the gallery for my students, how could I stay upset with you?"

Angela laughed. "I'm glad you came around to that idea. I was worried that only made it worse."

Stella looked into her drink, remembering how elated and on top of the world she'd felt the last time she was here drinking with Angela. Now, she felt more like she was trying to drown her sorrows as she took a long, deep sip of her margarita, downing almost half in one go. Angela's eyes went wide.

"Woah, all right. I didn't know that was the kind of night we were having, but I'm down." She flagged down the bartender and ordered two shots of tequila, which came with a salt rim and a lime wedge. Stella took hers with a grimace.

"Things have just been a little tough, lately. I'm enjoying the outlet to sort of get my mind off everything."

Angela frowned. "Tough how?"

"I don't think I've had enough drinks to talk about that, yet."

At that, Angela gave a wicked smile and waved the bartender over once more.

By the time two additional hours had passed, Stella had drunk so much that she was absolutely sure she would be more hungover tomorrow than she'd been since she was in her twenties. Angela was keeping pace, but seemingly much better at holding her liquor than Stella was, because while she herself felt positively drunk, Angela seemed relatively normal, if a little wobbly on her feet.

"Interested in talking to me about what's got you so down, now?" she asked after Stella's fourth shot of the night, and she sighed.

"I don't want to be a downer." Her words were a little slurred, but still comprehensible. Under an expectant stare, she caved. "It's just been hard. My classes aren't going so well, and I'm not selling paintings like I used to."

"I thought you just sold one to Andrew for a good chunk of money."

"I did!" she chirped, then frowned. "But that's the most I've made in a long time. My monthly income is coming, like, dangerously close to my expenses. I'm afraid..."

"What, Stella? What are you afraid of?"

"I'm afraid I just don't know how to do this. Maybe I just got lucky with all the success I've had."

"Well, that's ridiculous," Angela dismissed. "I've seen your work. I chose to do a gallery with you. That wasn't luck. You're talented, Stella." She sighed. "Look, I know things didn't go so well in Seattle, but my offer still stands. I'm not looking to push you into doing anything you're uncomfortable with. I have setups like this with a couple of artists. Think of it like a franchise. You'd run your location, make all the business decisions for yourself. Nothing would happen that you're against."

For once, Stella was speechless. Angela always found ways to surprise her. On paper, this was an incredible idea, wasn't it? The thought of owning a successful gallery, one with constant promotion by a famous artist she had once admired, selling her art for prices she couldn't dream of asking for here in Sunrise Beach... Wasn't that everything she wanted?

If it sounded so amazing, why was the voice in her head screaming at her not to do it?

"I'll think about it," she finally said, not knowing how she would even begin to open her mind.

Making Big Decisions

When the taxi dropped Stella off at her home that evening, she was more than a little tipsy. It didn't matter, she told herself. The house was all hers tonight, anyway, so what was the harm in falling asleep on the couch tonight and waking up tomorrow with a raging headache and a lot of regret?

"Mom?" Kelsey's voice startled her so badly when she stepped into the living room that she jumped.

"You scared the life out of me!"

Kelsey squinted. "Are you drunk? You smell like alcohol."

"I went out," she replied. "I didn't think you were going to be home."

"Of course I am," she snapped.

"You were so late, and you didn't even text. Do you know how irresponsible that is? I had no idea where you were. I was nervous. We have a deal, remember? You come home on weekends and breaks. What, did you and Marco have a fight? Is that why you came home?"

"What? No. His car broke down on the side of the road. We had to walk, like, three miles to a shop to get it fixed."

Stella felt a little guilty for snapping, but at the same time, she was furious at the fact that Kelsey hadn't thought to call. She was on that stupid cell phone all the time. How difficult could it have been to send her a quick update to let her know she was going to be late?

"I would have waited up if I knew you were coming home."

"It's fine." Kelsey stood, clearly having been hoping for a

different response. Stella was, too. After all, this was partially Kelsey's fault.

Kelsey could sense there was more Stella wanted to say. If her inhibitions were at their full capacity, she would have made a different choice. She wasn't even sure that she wanted to make such a big, radical change, but she couldn't get the thought out of her mind that this was the only decision that made sense.

"What?" Kelsey demanded, and she finally crumbled.

"I think we need to move again."

"What? Why?"

She sighed. How could she even begin to explain that this place was too small, that she'd outgrown it already and that if she didn't get out soon, she never would?

"You know how goldfish only grow to the size of their enclosures?" she asked. "If you keep one in a tiny bowl, it'll stay small, but if you put it in a pond, it'll grow to be enormous."

"I don't know if that's true or not," Kelsey admitted, "but I do remember you used to read me a story like that. It was like a little kid's book."

"Exactly. I think... I think maybe I need to move out of here if I want to keep growing."

Saying it aloud made it so much more real, and for a moment, she was just as speechless as Kelsey seemed to be. She watched her daughter staring at her with wide-eyed... something. Was that horror, or anger? Maybe just shock?

"I'm going to bed. It's late. Make sure you take off your makeup before you go to sleep."

"I'm not drunk." It was as much a defensive statement as it was a true one. As much as she wanted to make Kelsey see this from her perspective, she also could sense just how much anger was pent up there at having been accused of trying to break their deal, so she held her tongue as she watched her daughter stomp off to her room, then heard her slam the door behind her.

Just as she predicted, she woke the next morning feeling awful. Stella's head was throbbing, and her stomach felt unsettled. More than that, though, she felt run-down, exhausted like she'd been running a marathon. All her muscles ached, and when she sat up in bed and had to clutch one temple to stop the world from spinning, she was sure that she was more than just hungover. She was definitely overtired, probably even coming down with something.

She groaned as she stood slowly, gripping the wall for a moment until she felt steady enough to get to the bathroom to brush her teeth. A shower wasn't even worth trying today. When she finished, trying to part her hair in a way that made her look a little more put-together before heading to the kitchen, Kelsey was already sitting up and drinking coffee.

"There you are," she greeted irritably. "I was wondering when you were getting up."

Stella looked at the clock and winced—it was well past 9:00 a.m. "Sorry," she said. "I'm not feeling the best."

"I imagine not. Coffee's in the brewer, if you want it." Though her stomach said no, her tired mind said yes, so she poured herself a cup and sat down at the table. "I want to talk about last night."

Stella groaned again. "Oh, no."

"I'm not moving anywhere." Stella opened her mouth to argue, but Kelsey cut her off. "Let me finish. I know you said you have to get out of here because of your art career, and that's fine." Stella didn't miss the break in her voice, the disappointment at the idea Stella might be leaving. "But I just got comfortable here. I can't uproot my life again."

"I know. I just can't give up my passion. Honestly, I should have waited to have this conversation until I was sure, but I'm trying to figure things out, myself. I can't leave you, but I also couldn't live with myself if I sold myself short. That's what I've been doing all my life, and if I move somewhere else, I obviously can't keep paying for the cottage here."

"Well, I'm not leaving. I can't. I'll find some way to stay here, even if you're not going to."

After she stormed off, Stella immediately called Felicia, knowing that she would pick up the phone, and grabbed her purse before even waiting for a reply.

Chapter Nineteen

When the meeting with Felicia didn't go as planned, Stella was left with no choice but to call the only other person in her phone who she thought might pick up and understand —Angela Goff.

"I told my friend about what happened with Kelsey, and she was completely on her side. She acted like I was selling my soul to the devil by considering going into business with someone else."

"I don't think you're a sellout just for trying to get what you deserve," Angela said. "Just like any other career, you want to move up. You'd have to be stupid to pass up a good opportunity just because you don't want to let others lift you up."

Feeling heard and understood in a way that she hadn't in a while, Stella agreed to another trip to Seattle that night, and by the following Monday, she was hopping off a plane with Angela, this time with her own luggage in tow. Angela had been clear about not talking business with anyone

Stella might find untrustworthy this time, swearing that this visit was entirely for Stella's benefit. While her goal last time had been to show Stella what it took to be an artist in the big city, now, she was attempting to convince her of all the reasons that it was worth it.

"I had a lot more galleries that I wanted to show you before you left last time. We went to the big ones, but I should have brought you to the smaller ones owned by individuals. That's what you need to see—little, self-made artists thriving and living their best lives. They're totally inspiring."

Stella tried to get excited about this trip. After all, she'd been the one who had come to Angela and told her that perhaps she'd been too hasty in her judgment when she was first here. Angela had gone through all the trouble of arranging another trip, so the least she could do was enjoy it.

The problem was that as much as she wanted this trip to feel different from the last, she found that it just... didn't. That familiar frustration of not feeling the way she wanted to about something reared its ugly head. She remembered it well, from all the boys she'd wanted to return romantic feelings for in middle school to wanting to be interested in her father's great love of mathematics. All she wanted was to be impressed and at ease and feel like she belonged here, but it wasn't coming easily. The apartments Angela showed her were gorgeous, but the prices were absolutely astronomical.

"There's no way I could afford something like this," she reminded Angela. Thinking back to the divorce settlement, normally she'd have been entitled to a good deal of her and Jeff's income, but because Jeff's had been fraudulent, she'd been left with only the little savings she'd been able to prove were her own, and those had long since run out. She was able to comfortably pay her mortgage for the cottage, but something like a high-end apartment in a major city was certainly out of reach.

"But," Angela said, "you would. If you moved out here, gave yourself a real chance."

It was supposed to be an empowering trip, but if she were being honest, Stella began to feel more hollow the more time she spent in Seattle. It wasn't the same discomfort she'd felt the first time she came here, but an emptiness, a sense of resignation and loss. If she moved here, she would lose her daughter in a physical sense. Kelsey had made it very clear that she wasn't planning to move with her, and she wasn't sure if Felicia would want to keep in contact. Kelsey had been so angry when Stella proposed the idea of leaving, that she was positive that if she moved, she'd be burning the bridge forever. On top of that, she would have to abandon the gallery in Sunrise Beach, the place where she got her start and the first thing she'd ever truly built for herself. Would it hurt to abandon that?

"Stella," Angela called, sensing her sudden change of demeanor and pulling her from her thoughts. "What would you say to lunch?"

The spot Angela brought her to was quiet and secluded, a far cry from anywhere she'd taken her on their last trip. It was well-lit, and the menu was small, simple, and full of comfort foods that Stella found easy to crave. She ordered a grilled chicken sandwich with a side of french fries, while Angela had her typical salad. It wasn't so much a vacation for Angela, she remembered, as it was a work trip.

"You know, I think we're more alike than you think. I understand why you think I don't get you, or that your life and mine are so different, but I really do understand what drives you. I think it's time you understood me."

Stella wasn't sure what to say. "Of course," she replied, suddenly embarrassed. Had she really occupied that much of the conversation for the duration of their friendship? "You can tell me anything."

"I was married once."

"I'm sorry, but I... already knew that. It's not exactly a secret, is it? You've been pretty open."

Angela laughed. "I know, but you haven't let me finish. I met him in college. He was a writer, a poet. I thought he was my other half. We spent a wonderful year together, and on Christmas Day, he proposed to me. I said yes, obviously, because I thought at the time he was the love of my life."

"But he wasn't, I'm guessing?"

A faraway look took over Angela's eyes. "I wouldn't say that. If I could have spent my life with any one man, it would have been him. He was kind and brilliant and talented, and he loved me so much."

"So, what happened? I mean, I feel rude asking, but—"

"No, of course not. It's the point of this whole tale, after all, isn't it?" she laughed slightly, nostalgic but without a hint of melancholy. "It's not that he wasn't right for me. It's that I wasn't right for marriage. He wanted the whole nine yards. Kids, a dog, a little white picket fence. I couldn't give up my budding art career. Just before our anniversary, I sold my first painting, and that same day, I went down to my lawyer's office and served him papers."

Stella was, not for the first time in Angela's presence, stunned into silence. She couldn't imagine feeling that way about her life. Kelsey was the greatest thing that had ever happened to her. As much as she loved her art career, if she had to choose between it and raising her daughter, she'd have selected Kelsey every time, no hesitation. There was no amount of happiness she could sacrifice that wouldn't have been eclipsed by the vast, overwhelming love she held for her daughter, and that never would have happened without her marriage to Jeff. In her darkest moments, those when she began to regret having met him at all, she remembered that.

"I want to ask you again to go into business with me. I know you've had some wine, so I'm not asking tonight, but I made an appointment tomorrow at the bank to take out the loan for the rental space. I'll text you the address. The teller will be waiting for us, and I'm really hoping that you'll sign with me. What do you say? Will you be there?"

Though she knew in her heart what she really wanted, she could do nothing but nod. Tomorrow, she thought, her head would be clear and her path would reveal itself.

The next morning at nine, which was early for Angela but well after Stella's morning jog and shower, they met at the local bank. As Angela had promised, the teller was waiting there with paperwork for her.

"Good morning, ladies," he greeted, his eyes shining with anticipation. Stella almost felt a little guilty—surely, this guy was excited about the commission he thought he was about to make. "Can I get you some coffee?"

Stella shook her head, but Angela accepted the offer, though she turned her nose up when she smelled the aroma wafting from the Styrofoam cup. "Hey, Phil," Angela greeted. "Do you have the loan paperwork ready to go?"

He smiled. "Of course! I cleared my whole morning for it. I know it's going to seem like a lot, but I promise I'll walk you through it all. Ready?"

Stella was silent as she followed Angela to the man's desk, where he began to go through the details of a large stack of paperwork. It brought back memories of meetings she'd sat in on with Jeff, though of course, this was likely a lot less fraudulent. He talked about credit, how it wouldn't matter about the hit that Stella's had taken after the divorce because Angela's was so pristine. She watched as Angela signed document after document, initialing each page with growing anticipation.

"Okay, now, this is the very last one, and Ms. Britton, this is the one you're going to have to sign, too. It's basically just a commitment. For the next five years, you'll be on this lease. Ms. Goff is putting up the collateral, but you'll be equal partners."

Angela leaned toward Stella. "Don't let him scare you," she reassured. "I know it'll be profitable. We'll make enough to start covering our rent as soon as we get some art on those walls, so it won't be a problem."

When Angela offered the pen to her, Stella couldn't bring herself to take it, and she felt it pressed into her hand, the papers slid in front of her by Phil. For a long moment, she just stared at it, willing the words to look more appealing than they were. A five-year contract, practically guaranteed to be successful. A big city, a new start, her career finally valued by someone she admired greatly. Why couldn't she bring herself to press the pen to the page?

"I'm so sorry, Angela," she apologized, setting the pen back down in front of her. "I just can't do it. I want to want this, but it's just too much to give up. I need to stay in town with my daughter, my home. I know you gave those things up for your career, but my career means nothing to me without them. I hope you can understand."

She didn't dare look at the bank teller, but Angela's face fell so dishearteningly that it almost convinced her to sign, anyway, despite herself.

"Well, I wish I were more surprised," she sighed. "You have a lot of talent, Stella. A lot. I've never met another artist like you. I really hope that you're not making a huge mistake here."

Stella chuckled. "Yeah, me, too." She sighed. "I can't even begin to thank you for everything you've done for me. You've been an incredible mentor and an even better friend. I hope you'll allow me to keep in touch."

Angela's nod could have been sincere or polite, Stella couldn't tell. Instead of sticking around to try to decipher it, she picked up her purse and flagged down a cab to drive her back to the hotel, where she packed up her things and prepared to leave. There was a good chance she was leaving her friendship with Angela here in Seattle, but it was better than signing herself up for a long lease that would keep her from her child. Though she took the plane back home alone, she felt less isolated than she had in a long time, knowing that she was going back home to her community and friends. Felicia and Kelsey would both be happy she'd turned down the offer and, with any luck, accept her back with open arms.

Chapter Twenty

Stella didn't even bother to stop at home first on her way back from the airport. Her first and only priority was reaching her daughter. She knew that Kelsey would be at Marco's place right now, and perhaps she would hate the intrusion, but the way she'd left things had been rough. Kelsey was still angry, and definitely assuming that she'd gone to Seattle to sign the contracts and never come back. When Stella had reached out to a real estate agent about selling the cottage, she had been sure that Kelsey would never speak to her again.

Stella dragged her luggage into the lobby of Marco's apartment building, wishing she'd thought this through a little more. Ultimately the only important thing was to talk to her daughter and the plan to do that had been secondary. She considered hauling her bags up the stairs and discarded that idea in a split second. Looking around for a safe spot, she tucked her bags into a corner of the lobby and headed up the stairs to the third floor hoping nobody would bother it.

Kelsey was the one to answer the door when she knocked, dressed in sweatpants and a t-shirt that she was sure belonged to Marco. She tried not to wince at how close they had become.

"Mom?" Kelsey asked, not even bothering to veil her anger. "What are you doing here? I thought you were in Seattle."

"I was," she said. "I needed to see you."

"What, did the house sell or something? I told you, I'm not moving. I don't care what that real estate agent says—"

"No, just—please listen to me. Can I come in so we can talk?"

Kelsey hesitated, chewing on her bottom lip as she thought, then threw open the door without waiting for her mother to follow. Stella shut the door behind her, then sat down on the couch beside Kelsey. The apartment was small, its walls a boring white, minimally decorated. All their furniture looked inexpensive or damaged in one way or another, but still, it made her smile.

"Wow, this reminds me a lot of the first apartment I shared with your father. It was in a part of downtown Atlanta you've certainly never seen, the cheapest neighborhood we could find. We loved it. Do you like it here?"

Kelsey shrugged. "I'm hoping to start moving some of my things over here sometime, I guess. It doesn't feel like home."

Stella could read between the lines. "I didn't sell the cottage."

"So, what, you're going to commute? Kind of crazy, don't you think?"

"Honey, I'm so sorry for everything that happened. I didn't sign the paperwork."

Kelsey's jaw almost dropped. "You're not going into business with Angela?"

"No. I wanted to. Believe me, I felt terrible about going all the way out there and doing that to her again, but I just couldn't do it."

"What changed?"

Stella shrugged. "I guess I just realized it's not what I wanted. I would miss this place too much. I'd miss you too much. You're what's most important to me, and I love our home here, and my gallery."

Of course, it wasn't so easy to sway her smart, skeptical daughter with words alone. "So, what changed, then? You weren't so sure about that a week ago. How do I know you're not going to change your mind again the next time someone comes around with a shiny new opportunity?"

"I understand," she sighed. "I'm sorry for searching for greener pastures and not appreciating what I already have. We both worked so hard to accept this place, and now that we love it, I tried to leave. It wasn't fair to you."

"But is it really what you want?" Kelsey asked. "Are you giving up your dreams just to be here with me?"

"Angela told me that she realized that her calling was art because she was trying to connect with her husband, trying to want a child. I realized that my calling is art because you, our home, the things I love inspire my art. I couldn't be an artist without you. I'm not giving up anything."

Kelsey smiled, still guarded but softening. "I'll be home this weekend. We can talk about it then."

Home, Stella repeated in her mind. The word filled her with a sense of relief. How could she have taken it for granted? She'd almost made the biggest mistake of her life by giving it all up hoping for more.

She was surprised to know that the taxi driver hadn't left, so she didn't have to worry about calling another as she loaded her luggage back into the trunk and rode her way across town to her cottage once more, this time eager to see it again.

———

Perhaps because she was inspired, or maybe because she simply felt too tired to unpack her things, Stella tossed her bags into the bedroom and headed up to her studio. She was surprised that she even kept supplies in there anymore for how little she used it, but for some reason, she'd never found the strength to transfer her paints and canvases to the gallery. Just as well, she thought now—it wasn't as if she had any students to use them.

She began to dispense colors she didn't often use. Instead of her usual ocean blues and sunrise yellows, she mixed soft pinks, whites, pastel greens and purples. She agonized over the brown paint until it was the exact shade of Kelsey's hair, the blue until it matched her own eyes. Normally, on the very rare occasions she painted portraits of people, usually for her classes, she worked from a photograph. This time, however, the picture was vivid in her mind. It was a portrait of her and Kelsey, arm in arm, looking at one another with familial love and trust in their eyes. For the first time, she was sure that Kelsey fully trusted her to provide the stability and happiness she'd been afraid they'd lost forever after Jeff was arrested.

This portrait was not going to be sold—it would be too personal. She wanted to hang it on her own wall, feeling as though it would be a bit strange to have a picture of herself and her beautiful daughter adorning the wall of another person's home. However, as she painted, it did give her an idea. If her students were starting to tire of painting landscapes and still life, perhaps she could offer a course on portraiture. It could drive up her enrollment as well as help her to practice a skill she had hardly used since she was taking painting lessons herself.

When Stella pitched the idea of a figure-painting class to Merry and the rest of the college art department board, they loved it immediately.

"I was thinking that we could do a segment on family," she explained. "We could advertise it as a way to make some really good gifts for family members a few months before the holidays. I could do classes on proportion and expression and movement in art. I think it could be really successful, if you're willing to give me a chance."

Merry seemed to think it over, and there was a long moment where Stella wasn't sure if her previous resignation was going to be counted against her. She had, after all, been so disappointed when she'd confessed that she was probably moving and going to be unable to teach another class in the following semester. However, after a long moment, Merry grinned.

"I think it's a lovely idea," she said. "People love figure painting. They want to paint their loved ones. We could get a lot of people to sign up for something like that, I think. Plus, it's such a high-level skill, it'd need a whole series of classes!"

Stella let out a breath she hadn't known she was holding, feeling relieved. "I'll do some promotion on my website. Maybe we can draw some more people from my private classes into the college. I think it might be good to consolidate, if I'd be teaching more classes here."

Merry nodded. "Well, we would certainly love that. We could talk about a commission rate, too, if it turns out to be a real success. I have to ask, though—the last time we spoke, you seemed pretty dead set on leaving for bigger and better things. You said you were going to move to a big city and start a gallery. What changed?"

She'd expected the question, and when she'd tried to come up with a good answer to it in the car on the way here, Stella had drawn nothing but blanks. It seemed like nothing had changed, but everything, all at the same time.

"I think what you really want to know is whether I'm here for good," she said, maintaining eye contact with a sense of confidence she hadn't expected. "And to that, I can promise that I am. All I want is to be a successful artist, and I've been trying to figure out what that means to me. What I've realized is that I need to define that for myself, not measure myself next to others. Teaching makes me happy, so I want to keep doing it, if you'll let me."

Making Big Decisions

Angela and her friends had looked down on this position. "Those who can't do, teach," Angela had joked at her more than once, but Stella had never felt that way. To her, those who want to encourage a new generation of doers, who wanted to see more beauty in the world and inspire more people of all ages to chase their dreams—that was the real measure of a successful artist. All she wanted to do was be happy, and if she could teach what she knew to others to help them achieve their dreams as well, then she would count herself lucky.

After the meeting let out, Stella followed Merry to her office to discuss the particulars of the classes she would be teaching. They would start within a few weeks, which was a tight deadline, but Stella supposed she'd been asking for it, since she'd taken so much time off lately thinking that she was going to give all this up and move away. The college couldn't stop its schedule just because she had an identity crisis. Stella promised that she could get it done, not really caring about how much work it might be. In fact, she was a little excited. Curriculum design was fun for her.

Because Felicia was friends with another member of the staff at the college, Stella knew that the news she was rejoining the team would make it to her. They hadn't spoken since she'd left for Seattle, and with the way they'd left things, Stella hadn't been entirely sure she would want to hear from her when she returned. Felicia had been so disappointed and angry when she'd heard the news, Stella didn't know if their friendship would survive what Felicia had taken as a personal betrayal.

For that reason, Stella was surprised when her phone

buzzed in her pocket that evening, hours after she'd finished her discussion with Merry. She had gone home and poured herself a glass of wine, her luggage still sitting in the living room. Unpacking it just sounded too exhausting at the moment.

"Hey," read the text message. She waited for a follow-up, but none came. She rolled her eyes, but felt a sudden pang of anxiety in her chest. What if she were texting to say that something had happened?

"Hi," Stella replied. "Everything okay?"

"I heard you came back to S. B. Is that true?"

"Just call me," she replied, and though she only half expected her to do it, she picked up when her phone began to ring. "I didn't think you'd call. I know how angry you are with me."

Felicia sighed. "I'm sorry about that. I don't think it was terribly fair. I'm not upset any longer." A pause. "So, did you do it? Sign the papers, I mean. Are you going into business with Angela Goff?"

"No. I realized that we're too different. I love teaching, and even if my gallery is small and nameless forever, it's mine. I built it myself, and I'm really proud of it. At least for now, I'm not looking to make any big changes to my life."

Felicia's entire tone shifted from tentative and guarded to elated. "I'm so thrilled to hear that, Stella! Really, I am. I knew you'd come to your senses. I just knew it."

She tried not to flinch at the implication that what she'd done had been so crazy. "I just needed a little time to figure out who I am and what I want, you know?"

Making Big Decisions

"I'm sorry for overreacting. I just... I don't often have girlfriends, and I was really afraid of how much I'd miss you. Not only that, but I know you. The way you talk about Atlanta, the big city and all... I know you wouldn't be happy there again."

"That's not—that isn't why I was unhappy in Atlanta. There was a lot more to it than that."

"Was there?" she asked. "You told me you hated the people you had to pretend to be friends with for your husband's sake. Do you really think that would be different if you were rubbing elbows with people to advance your own career rather than Jeff's?"

"I wouldn't do that."

"You would, because you'd have to. It'd be the only way to nudge out the competition, and believe me, in a city like that, there would be a lot of competition. People like Angela who are doing anything they need to do to get ahead of hardworking, talented people like yourself. Here, everyone supports your career. Everyone here loves you. We want to see you thrive."

Stella felt as though she could cry. She really had almost made a huge mistake. Felicia was right—she would be unhappy having to deal with the cutthroat nature of an art career in an artist's city. She'd already lived a life where every action she took was scrutinized by others, where she had to be polite to the right people even when they were unkind to her, and spend dinners with folks she hated. Doing that again would have made her miserable. There was no amount of success in her art career that would be worth that.

"In any case," Felicia continued, "I'm just glad to hear

you turned her down. I think that deserves a drink. Want to come over?"

Despite how exhausted Stella felt from the plane ride and the long meeting, even knowing how much work she had ahead of her with her new classes about to start and having had no time to prepare for them, she grinned.

"I would love nothing more. I'll be over in twenty."

Chapter Twenty-One

The new semester began. Stella had been optimistic about how many people might be interested, but even so, she was shocked to hear that every single slot in her new classes were full. And the wait list was so long that it practically guaranteed another semester of full enrollment at least. She never would have guessed that so many people would be interested in learning from her. It had taken a lot of work to get her curriculum ready before the deadline, but she'd just managed it.

One of the best things about working for the college was that she was able to have lunch with Kelsey on the occasions when the gap in her classes and Kelsey's lined up. It happened about once a week, if Kelsey wasn't busy with homework or something for her internship. It made the fact that Stella no longer saw her during the week a little easier to handle, since she now had more than just two days to catch up with her. All the things she would have forgotten about if she waited until Saturday—minor annoyances from the internship, arguments she had with her friends, fun facts she learned in class—Stella loved hearing all of it. This was exactly the kind of thing she would miss out on if she had made the decision to move to Seattle.

"The holiday is coming up," Kelsey pointed out over two mediocre hamburgers from the cafeteria. "Is Grandma going to come visit?"

"I don't think so," Stella admitted. "I think your dad is going to get furlough, but he obviously won't be able to come all the way up here to visit. He'll have to stay within a certain distance of the prison. Do you want to go see him?"

Kelsey shook her head. "I don't think I'm ready for that yet."

"Okay. I just thought I'd offer. You're going to come home then, right?"

"I was actually hoping to talk to you about that. I know I told you I'd spend the breaks with you instead of Marco, but he's got nowhere to go for Christmas. I just feel so bad that he's going to spend the whole time all alone."

"You're asking to stay there instead?"

"Well," she hesitated," I was actually hoping that maybe he could come stay with us. He could sleep on the couch, if you don't want him in my room. I just think he'd have a good time being surrounded by family for once, you know? It's been years since he's had that."

Stella took a moment to think it over, knowing that her soft heart couldn't possibly deny her daughter her request. She remembered just how hard the first few years after her parents' passing were, especially around the holidays. There was no lonelier time than to not be surrounded by family for Christmas.

Making Big Decisions

"I think that's a great idea, actually. Invite him over. He can open his presents with us on Christmas Day instead of early or late depending on when I'd have gotten them to him. And we'll have more than enough food as usual. It'll be fun. Just ask him if he's got any food allergies and what he likes to drink."

Kelsey's eyes lit up. "Thank you, Mom! He's going to be so happy."

Though she was a little disappointed that the holiday wouldn't be just her and Kelsey anymore, Stella was happy about the chance to get to know Marco a little better. Not to mention, this was an excellent way to ensure that she kept Kelsey happy and close to home. If she said no, Kelsey would no doubt be leaving almost daily to go visit Marco and keep him company.

Luckily, Stella had gone ahead and bought an air mattress after Gwen had left. She'd had to see a chiropractor for two months to get all the kinks out of her spine from the weeks of sleeping on the couch, so she decided that was not a mistake she'd make again. Ultimately, after much debate, they decided to assemble the mattress in Stella's painting studio. Kelsey's room was not only too small to fit both, but Stella wasn't so keen on the idea of the two sharing a room under her roof, even if she did allow Kelsey to stay with Marco during the school year. Setting up the mattress in the living room would just be a hassle, not to mention the fact that it would give him no privacy to get dressed or to sleep in late if he wanted to. Stella didn't want to wake him over his holiday break by stepping over him to get to the door for her morning jog every day.

It had taken no small amount of effort to clean out the

studio enough to make it livable. Supplies had been everywhere, canisters of dried-up oil paints, bottles of solvent, and brushes littering the floor. She'd had to find a place for several unfinished paintings and several more that would likely never see the light of day. It was just so easy to begin a project, step away to allow the first layer to dry, and never pick it up again.

Kelsey helped her clear out the room, carting big boxes between home and her gallery. Boy, she sure was glad she didn't sell that. She'd be regretting it now. It took the better part of two days to be able to walk around freely, then another day to scrub the floor enough that it no longer smelled like wet paint, but when they finished, it could have almost passed as a guest bedroom.

"Do you think he'll be okay in here?" Stella asked. "I mean, if it's going to be a problem, we could figure something else out."

Kelsey's eyes wandered around the room, taking in the fruits of all their hard work, and smiled. "I think he'll love it, honestly. We're college students, Mom. This room is, like, nicer than half our friends' apartments." Stella laughed, but Kelsey shook her head. "I'm serious. I have a friend who doesn't even have furniture. When we hang out at his place, we all just sit on lawn chairs. This is practically luxurious compared to that."

She was right—Marco was nothing but appreciative of the room they had cleared out for him. He thanked Stella over and over for having him there for an entire month while the college was on break, promised not to be in the way, and offered to help with anything he could.

Making Big Decisions

"I'm not a very good cook," he started, and Kelsey snorted.

"That's an understatement."

"I'll try, though! And if not, I can go to the grocery store for you, or do the dishes. I just feel really bad about being a burden. I know it's Christmas, and you've probably got enough to do with your business."

This was a new side to Marco that Stella hadn't seen before, and she had to say she liked it. When he wasn't trying to be cool and impressive, he was actually a pretty timid, meek guy. She could see why Kelsey liked him.

"Don't worry about anything. I'm sure I'll find some way to keep you busy, but it's your winter break. I don't want to burden you. You kids work so hard at school these days. I see all the books Kelsey brings home, and I think it's just criminal how much homework you have. Just enjoy your break. You're not a bother here."

This speech, she was almost entirely stealing from her mother-in-law. When Stella had first moved in with Gwen and Jeff after her parents passed, she had been so afraid of being a burden. She'd felt for sure like the only people in her life that wanted to take care of her were gone, and Gwen was only offering to take her in because she felt badly for her. She didn't want pity, and had been not only slightly aggressive about that point, but had felt cripplingly guilty. For the first week, she'd woken up early to ensure she got to cook breakfast, and when she couldn't beat Gwen to starting dinner, she didn't let the dishes so much as touch the sink before she started washing them. She dusted, vacuumed, and scrubbed the bathroom with such frequency that Gwen had commented that it was beginning to feel more like a restaurant than a home.

"Honey," she'd told her at the time, "you need to slow down. This is the time to just let someone take care of you, okay? You're not a bother here."

She could tear up at the memory if she dwelled on it, so instead, she decided to turn her attention back to the task at hand, which was moving Marco's things into her old studio. Stella encouraged him to hang posters on the walls if he wanted to, which were bare now that she had taken down the paintings that had been hanging to dry. She cleared a bit of junk out of her dresser and lugged it up the stairs to give him a place to unpack his clothes, since he wouldn't have a closet, and showed him where the laundry room was. She reassured him that he didn't have to ask for anything he wanted from the kitchen, so long as he wrote an item on the grocery list if he used the last of it. Finally, they discussed the rules surrounding curfew. They could stay out in the living room until eleven p.m., and after that, they had to retreat to their separate bedrooms. Though Kelsey rolled her eyes through that part of the discussion, she didn't object, so Stella counted it as a win.

Within a few days, things began to settle down. Stella didn't feel as much anxiety as she had thought she would when she left the two of them alone in the house to go to her studio, and now that the college was on break, she had nothing but time for herself. She used it to start painting again, something she'd been neglecting a bit since she'd been so busy.

Having Marco around made her think even more

deeply about what family meant to her. For the longest time, she couldn't have painted anything relating to her family without Jeff. A portrait of herself and Kelsey would have felt like something, someone, was missing. It would have made her sad to look at. Now, however, things were a little different. Her days, even when Kelsey was out of the house, didn't feel lonely. Sure, she spent them alone, but it wasn't the crushing type of isolation that had haunted her for the first months of living in Sunrise Beach. It had taken her a long time to learn to sleep alone in her bed, but now, she loved having the whole thing to herself.

Without her even noticing, her definition of family had shifted. Rather than feeling like they were missing something vital, she began to feel whole again. When Kelsey had first started living most of her time at Marco's, she had felt a little empty, but slowly, she'd learned to enjoy her time alone almost as much as her time with Kelsey. That was how it was supposed to feel, she thought, as a child prepared to leave the nest. Those anxieties that had initially plagued her about whether Kelsey would be eating enough, if she'd be able to focus on her studies, if she would need her mother to swoop in and solve her problems—all of them were alleviated by the passage of time.

Each weekend, she would see Kelsey once more, very much alive, happy, and healthy. She'd ask her about her diet and learn that she and Marco had decided to subscribe to one of those meal kits that send ingredients for healthy dinners three times a week, and that the other two, they usually had leftovers, save for the occasional treat of takeout during a particularly busy week. She certainly wasn't allowing her grades to slip. Every problem she encountered, she was able to work out for herself. By trusting her daughter, she found that she was able to let go, and in doing so, she discovered a part of herself that she had never seen before.

After spending so many years defining herself as a mother first and foremost and a wife after that, she had lost what it meant to do things for herself. Everything she did was for Kelsey, whether it was chaperoning a school trip or making decorations for a class party. Everywhere she went was for Jeff, to visit people he needed to impress or to scope out new business ventures. She hosted dinners for people she'd never met, attended parties where all she did the entire night was sit alone in a corner and drink champagne, watching her husband impress his bosses. For a while, she'd even played tennis with Jeff's boss' wife in an attempt to edge out a coworker for a promotion. Nothing she had done in those times had been for herself, so much so that she'd forgotten that she could even live in a way that focused on her own wants and needs.

That was marriage and motherhood, though, wasn't it? At least, that had been what she'd always told herself. All her married friends seemed to live the same way. A good relationship took sacrifice. That had always been what she'd been told growing up, and she was willing to make them for Jeff because she'd taken for granted the idea that he would do the same for her. He had proven, however, that he wouldn't. He put their whole family in danger.

With Kelsey, things were different. It was never a bother to sacrifice, and she had never once felt as though the things she gave up for her daughter made her weaker or unhappy—on the contrary. Everything that she was able to do for Kelsey was worth any cost. It was just that now that she didn't need those things anymore, Stella had to readjust her worldview. Now she was able to start focusing on what she wanted, which was a question she hadn't asked herself since before she was married.

Marco was helpful around the house, and the way he interacted with Kelsey was sweet. He snuck her kisses on the cheek when he thought Stella wasn't looking, all of which were quickly and bashfully batted away by her daughter, who would have been mortified to know Stella thought it was cute. She began to paint the two of them together, sometimes, though she wouldn't tell Kelsey this. She didn't want her to think that she was beginning to believe that this was a forever relationship. She maintained that Kelsey and Marco were both too young to be thinking about that sort of thing, but when she saw the two of them together, drinking coffee at the kitchen table and laughing at some video on one of their phones, or attempting to follow a recipe together, or holding hands under the blankets while the three of them watched a movie—it was impossible not to feel like Marco was, at least for now, a part of the family.

Stella began working on a new piece. This one was her daughter and Marco sitting on the porch watching the sun set and sipping a Coke together, a scene she had accidentally stumbled upon one evening as she came in with groceries. She hadn't wanted to interrupt it because it made her heart feel so warm, but Marco had immediately jumped up to assist her with bringing the groceries inside and Kelsey was starving and wanted to start cooking. The tableau had remained with her, though. Something about having felt like she was responsible for ending the moment made her want to capture it in a portrait. Perhaps, if things worked out, she would have an occasion to show it to Kelsey someday, when the two were older and more mature.

Chapter Twenty-Two

The month of winter break felt like it flew past. Christmas day was more special than it had been in a long time. Marco hadn't opened presents from under the tree in years, so he was up at the crack of dawn, ready to go. He made a pot of coffee and surprised both Stella and Kelsey with a cup in bed, but really, it was just an excuse to get them up and going so he could open his gifts. He'd gotten Stella a set of paintbrushes—nice ones, too. They had pretty, decorative handles that she loved. She would feel too guilty using them and making them dirty, but she appreciated them, anyway.

After Christmas, things settled into a routine. Stella would leave for the studio in the morning to paint and run the gallery while Kelsey and Marco enjoyed their free time watching movies, going to the mall, or whatever else struck their fancy. Sometimes, Marco would get antsy, feeling cooped up in the house and tired of the beach he'd lived next to all his life, and come help Stella with the gallery. He did a lot of tasks that she couldn't, like standing on ladders to change light bulbs and carrying heavy boxes from room to room. More than that, though, he seemed to have a genuine interest in learning. Art wasn't exactly his thing, but she discovered quickly that what he did love was teaching. Stella could see the makings of a very good teacher in him, if he wanted to be.

"I've been wondering something," he asked one day while he helped her with her lesson plan. "Have you ever considered hiring more employees?"

Stella frowned. "I haven't," she admitted. "I've always just run the place by myself. It's never really needed any more than I could do, you know?"

"I guess. I was just thinking that with all you do now at the college, you could probably use a hand around here, don't you think?"

One side of her mouth quirked up. "Are you asking for a job?"

"I guess I am."

"Well then, Marco. When summer comes and you have some more free time, consider yourself my first employee."

Marco grinned.

———

When Stella returned home that evening, there was a stack of mail on the table. Marco had been bringing it inside for her, so she leafed through the envelopes of bills and coupons until she found something of interest. It was a letter that was hand-addressed to her, from England.

"Oh, no," she whispered to herself, feeling her heart take off. She took a steadying breath before tearing off the edge of the envelope. Inside was exactly what she imagined —a letter from Graham.

Dear Stella,

I'm writing to see how you've been getting on since we last spoke. I know we didn't leave things perfectly, but I still care about you. Felicia often tells me about how well you're doing and I think it's fantastic to hear. Your studio deserves success, even if that had taken you out of Sunrise Beach. Between you and me, however, I'm glad it didn't.

Things are going swimmingly here, which is to say that every day is the same, I suppose. I think of you often. The weeks we spent together were some of the only true fun I've had in ages. I wish I could come visit whenever I wanted, but unfortunately, it doesn't work like that.

If you'd like to keep in contact, even despite how strained things were between us when I had to leave, I'd love to hear back from you.

All my best,
Graham Townsend

Stella clutched the letter to her chest for a moment, fully indulging in how much of a dramatic cliché it was. It felt good to know he wanted her attention, wanted to hear from her. She couldn't believe how much of her story Felicia had told him, and she could only guess at how much more she'd gossiped about her.

Receiving this letter from Graham made her feel entirely different than the way she'd felt about Jeff's. When she'd gotten that one, she'd felt dread, and had replied out of a sense of obligation to the man she'd spent so many years married to. This letter made her feel excited. There were so many things she wanted to tell him, even if Felicia probably already had given away any surprises. She was curious to hear what he'd been up to, as well.

Without hesitation, Stella opened her laptop and started typing up a reply. Before she knew it, she'd already written an embarrassing number of pages, concerning the two disastrous trips to Seattle, how she'd almost sold her house and studio, and the fact that Kelsey's boyfriend was now their temporary house guest. She had even more questions for him. What was he doing? Were things going well with his new clients? How did he spend most of his time? And, of course, the question she wanted to ask more than any other but couldn't—was he seeing someone?

She reassured herself that she was only curious, that she'd have these questions for any friend she hadn't seen in months, but she knew she was lying to herself. She missed Graham, and a large part of her was tempted to tell him as much. Instead, she labored over a reply that was measured but interested, curious without sounding desperate.

Dear Graham,

I'm so happy to hear you're doing well. Yes, Kelsey and I have been busy. She's kicking butt in school, on track to be top of her class. Couldn't be more proud of her.

As for me, things have been confusing, but I think I'm figuring them out. I wish you were here. The stories I'd tell you—you'd laugh at me. A little teaser—I went to Seattle with Angela, bailed with a transparent lie, then went back, really thinking I was going to go into business with her. I can't believe myself sometimes! I'm just glad I didn't sign the contract. Sunrise Beach feels like home now.

I think of you, too, and always wish the best for you. Felicia's stories about what you're up to aren't enough. Why don't you call sometime? Or, better yet, make an excuse for a visit?

I know we didn't leave things perfectly, but I don't care about that anymore. What I know is that I care about you, and I hope you'll keep in contact. Be well, Graham. Call me.

Yours,
Stella

Normally, Stella wouldn't have had the confidence to tell him exactly how she felt, but she was still riding the high of her realization in Seattle. If she was going to start focusing on what she wanted with her life, she had to begin having the drive to pursue those things. It would be uncomfortable, and perhaps sometimes even frightening, but it was what she had to do if she was going to turn this life around and start living for herself.

She would start with her studio, ensuring that it was entirely her own, with no one else's hands in the pot, no one's opinions influencing what she could and couldn't hang on the walls.

From there... well, she supposed she would just have to wait and see. Instead of being anxious about what might or might not happen next, she was content. She was definitely looking forward to focusing on the journey. She prayed the journey would take her to places she was dreaming of going.

In Book Five - *Running to Happiness* - Stella takes big leaps to make everything in her life work again. Though the road isn't completely smooth and wonderful, Stella's positioned herself to overcome the troubles life throws at her.

Stella Britton and her daughter Kelsey are happy with their small beach town lives. There were many times when it seemed like happiness would never come and that makes today all the more precious.

Kelsey is happy, healthy, and her life is headed in an amazing direction. Stella couldn't be more pleased with how things have worked out for her beloved daughter. With all the struggles of starting her life over, making sure her daughter was settled has been a huge concern through it all.

Graham is a part of her life - if only on the fringes. England is a long way from Sunrise Beach and phone calls don't make up for seeing each other in person. Stella can't bring herself to push him away, though. There's something there even if it may never work out to be more than a long distance friendship.

In spite of all the good in her life, the past still nags at Stella. Her ex shows up from time to time and every time she sees him all the terrible things he did rush back and make her feel almost as lost as she did when she found out what he'd done. She knows he deserves a chance to rebuild the relationship with his daughter, but he doesn't deserve a chance with her.

When her ex springs new information on her, everything she's worked so hard for is threatened. Protecting her daughter and herself may turn out to be one of the hardest things she's ever done. The most painful part of it all is that her relationship with Graham - who had become her rock - might have to be sacrificed.

Grab your copy of Running to Happiness on Amazon to finish this series of starts and stops, growth and moving forward.

About the Author

Charlotte Golding has always loved women's fiction - she inherited that love from her mother. Actually, her love of reading started at an early age because her mom read to her every day. What an amazing legacy to instill a love of reading in your children.

Charlotte started out writing historical romance and enjoyed it so much. The research was fun, though there was always a rabbit hole to swallow her up. That's one of the truths of a historical writer.

The call of women's fiction wouldn't go away. So here she is, in the world of women's relationships, family drama, and strong female characters. And she loves it!

Charlotte is a southern girl at heart. She left the south at times over the years, but came back as soon as possible to the place she knows she belongs.

Made in the USA
Columbia, SC
06 March 2022